I0531603

# The Sword of Myralis
## Darkshield Volume III
### By Kathe Todd

# Chapter 1

Adara awoke in her big, comfortable bed on the second floor of Underhill, and squeezed her eyes tight shut. Tears leaked out, and she angrily rubbed her eyes to brush them away. Then she opened them again. There was just enough light in the room for her to see, though the sun had not yet risen.

Over the winter Malika had taken to sleeping every night in the kitchen, warm beside the bread oven and ready to jump up at a moment's notice should her sharp ears pick up the sound of mice. Caraline claimed she hadn't seen a mouse in the pantry since the semigryph had first taken up residence.

Adara reached out for her furry-and-feathery friend with her mind, and found her sleeping. As she herself should be. She was utterly alone, and had no plans for the day. Stellan was gone, as she had known for months he would one day be. They'd had some amazing times together since their adventure in the Siiri's underground city, exploring Rivermarch from one end to the other and venturing up into Northmarch in search of more ancient treasures. But whenever they returned to Underhill, to the place she had begun to think of as home, she had seen how he chafed to spend time with her family.

The Underhills' quiet farm life, which Adara saw as a refreshing refuge from her perilous adventures, Stellan had found oppressive and dull. There had been many tasks associated with preparing the world for the return of the kobolds as well, and while he'd been willing to help with them she had seen how little such activities appealed to him. He'd only been going along with what she wanted to do because he loved her, she guessed. But in the end, that love had not been strong enough.

Their sex life had been the most astonishing thing about their relationship – two people who were thoughtful, intelligent, and reserved, yet even after months together they could not keep their hands off each other. Only three days since Stellan had left, and already her loins ached with unfulfilled desire. He'd said he would be coming back, but Adara recalled she'd told Ferdyn the same thing. It had been most of a year since then, and here she was.

Adara lay beneath the covers with her eyes half-closed, musing about Ferdyn and the life she'd left behind in Carlienne. What was he doing now? Had he moved on? Surely, her departure from his life must have left a gap that dozens of beautiful, high-born women would have been happy to fill. Ferdyn was a hunk, handsome, charming, friendly, great in the sack – and filthy rich. What woman wouldn't die for the chance to get her claws into him?

Eyes wide open now, Adara sat up in bed. She had suddenly been seized with the desire to look in on Ferdyn, and it had just occurred to her there might be a way she could do that. Clad in a beautiful lacy nightdress, she made her way across the room to the sturdy oaken chest of drawers. Having a home base had meant being able to own more clothing than she could carry in a pack or strapped to Sadiq's back, and she now had many fine clothes.

In among the underthings in the top drawer, some of them lacy and others utilitarian, she rummaged to the bottom and found Fatiha Baba. She had acquired this enchanted necklace, which appeared to have consciousness as if it contained the soul of a sentient being, after killing the Mancer King Sarand Bloodspire not quite a year ago. In awe of its powers, she had tucked it away and not worn it since. Now she got it out of its hiding place, and clasped it around her neck.

Questing with her mind, Adara silently addressed the presence that lived within the magical artifact. "Fatiha Baba, I would speak with you."

"*I am at your command,*" came the telepathic reply.

"Tell me of yourself, and of your powers," she commanded it. "Can you open a portal for me to anywhere?"

"Long ago my master Satar Adeem bound me in this form, so that I might serve his needs and those of his descendants," the spirit replied. "My kind are what you humans call djinni, inhabitants of the spirit plane who can manifest here in the physical plane if summoned by magic."

A djinn! Adara had heard of these. The magic practiced by inhabitants of the Sultanate of Khouresh, east of the Crestan range that divided the continent, was said to make use of the powers of these spirits who, from the description, seemed similar to the elemental spirits she herself could call on. They had great powers, but were in many ways like capricious children. Yet apparently the Khoureshi magi could bind the djinni to their will, even force them to remain in the physical plane. "And as to the portals?" she prodded.

"My ability to open doors is dependent on the mind of the one who controls me," Fatiha Baba explained. "If you can form a detailed mental picture of the place you wish to go, I can open a door to it. The size of the portal will be determined by the power of your mind. For you, I can open one large enough to transport an army."

Wow, Adara thought. Now *that* was a vote of confidence from a supernatural being who ought to know! But it sounded as if she would be able to open a door only to places she had been before, ones she knew well. That ruled out exploring the world – or alternate dimensions like the world of the Swinzen – using Fatiha Baba's power. But she should certainly be able to use it to return home, or to visit other places she had been, provided she'd been able to fix them in her mind.

She called up a vision of the bedchamber she had shared with Ferdyn at his opulent townhouse in the Palace District of Carlienne. She had slept there every night for nearly two months, after all. "Fatiha Baba, open a portal here," she commanded while keeping her mental picture sharp. "Just big enough for me to step through," she added.

Abruptly a rectangular hole a little bigger than a normal doorway appeared in the air between Adara and the chest of drawers. Through it, she could dimly see the bed and some of the furnishings of the room she had pictured in her mind. It was still the wee hours of the morning in Carlienne, many miles to the west; but the Palace District had streetlamps and it was never completely dark there. Taking a deep breath, Adara stepped through.

# Chapter 2

Barefoot on the thick Khoureshi carpet, Adara padded soundlessly toward the enormous four-poster bed with its lavish canopy. This far into spring it was not that cold on the coast, and Ferdyn was sleeping with the bedcurtains tied up. She peered down at him. He was sleeping alone!

She had only intended to look in on him unawares, to see how he was doing, to confirm her expectation that he'd moved on. After all, she'd been wrapped in the arms of another lover for months. Once she'd seen him, she would be able to put him out of her mind. But there he was alone, and looking as beautiful as ever in the dim light from the bedroom windows.

"Please close the portal, Fatiha Baba," Adara sent silently. The rectangle, which from where she stood showed a much brighter view of her bedroom at Underhill, vanished from view. Reaching up, Adara pulled her nightdress off over her head and let it drop to the floor. Then she slipped naked into bed beside Ferdyn, excitement and joy rising.

He was deeply asleep, and only roused slightly as his former lover squeezed up behind him and put an arm around his waist. He was wearing underdrawers but nothing else, and she gently stroked his chest and belly. Surprisingly, the life of leisure and luxury he'd chosen had not left Ferdyn the worse for wear. His abdominal muscles were still firm and well-defined, smooth skin overlying them without a trace of excess fat.

Adara's hand went lower, finding his cock beneath the underdrawers and stroking gently. It twitched and began to respond, stiffening swiftly as her ministrations appeared to have triggered a sexual dream. Ferdyn mumbled softly, and his own hand went down to his crotch. Suddenly his eyes flew open. There was someone in bed with him!

He seized her wrist, and rotated until he was facing her, blinking in the dim light. "Adara...?" he breathed in disbelief. Was it just a vivid dream? She pressed herself against him, breasts to naked chest, and gave him a sweet kiss.

"I was missing you, sweetie," she murmured.

6

Mind in a daze, Ferdyn kissed her back. If this was only a dream, it was one he'd thought about dozens of times over the months since Adara had left his side. Pretty women were a shilling a dozen in the capital, but it was she who haunted him.

Ferdyn threw the covers down off of them, gazing in wonder at this vision who'd appeared in his bed. He reached out tentatively and gently squeezed a breast. It certainly *felt* real. She put her hand into the fly of his drawers and winkled out his cock, which was now full-on hard, and gave it a much firmer squeeze. *That* felt real, too!

What the hell, go for it. He hoped he wasn't going to wake up in the morning in a pool of semen. Ferdyn cupped her chin with his free hand and covered her mouth in a deep kiss, tongue going inside. It felt, it tasted like Adara. Oh please, don't let this be a dream, he pleaded to whatever god might care to answer his prayer.

In moments his drawers had been pulled off and tossed to the floor beside the bed, and he was inside her. Oh yes, yes! This was the woman he'd taught to make love, the woman he had fallen in love with within days of their first meeting. It was not in his nature to sink into despair over a lost love, and over the months since she'd left him he had mostly gotten over his hurt. But to have her in his bed again!

They climaxed together, and Adara did not dissolve into mist as Ferdyn had half expected. She still appeared to be real and solid, sighing softly as she tucked herself beneath his arm and idly stroked his chest. Finally, he couldn't stand it any longer. "Adara, how… why…?" he managed to get out, and she smiled up at him lazily like the cat that got the cream.

"Do you remember Fatiha Baba?" she asked softly. Ferdyn heaved himself up in bed and looked around the room. It looked the same as it always did. Adara had explained about the consciousness residing in the Mancer King's magic necklace, and that it had a name. But she had never tried to use it after they'd closed that portal to the world of the Swinzen, back last summer.

After Adara had explained how she came to be here, it was her turn to get some answers. "Please don't tell me you've been pining away in an empty bed since I left," she said. Ferdyn chuckled, and squeezed her.

"Me, celibate?" he snorted. "I'm the most eligible bachelor in Carlienne at the moment. This bed has seen a lot of action since last year. But I don't let them spend the night. Nobody I've met could take your place. Besides, why tie myself down with one woman when there are dozens after my ass?"

While the part about nobody he'd met being able to take Adara's place sounded nice, the rest of that statement was a little off-putting. But she got a grip on her feelings. She liked Ferdyn, she was hugely attracted to him and loved having sex with him. But he wasn't the love of her life, or anything like that – any more than Stellan had been.

Was she incapable of the kind of romantic love that would make her want to settle down with one man and have his babies, Adara wondered? It made her a little sad to consider that. If true, it might lead to her having a lonely old age. But she had only recently turned eighteen. Old age was a long way off, yet. Maybe she just hadn't yet met The One. She did love Ferdyn, she thought. But it was more the love you would feel for a good friend.

They talked quietly for some time, Adara catching Ferdyn up on her remarkable discovery of a living mother and other relatives in Willoughby, and her adventures over the past few months. None of the later ones had quite matched their search for the tomb of the kobold king in intensity, but most of them had resulted in new knowledge and valuable plunder. She'd let Stellan keep most of the latter – he certainly needed it more than she did.

While Adara had been busy with all that Ferdyn had discovered the hobby of participating in the tourneys that were thrown in the capital several times a year, which accounted for his having stayed in shape. These mock battles offered some of the excitement of his former life as an adventurer, but without any of the hardship and with relatively little danger. King Arden, pleased with his prowess, had knighted him and he was now "Sir Ferdyn." Adara marveled.

Dawn was beginning to light the sky to the east, and at Underhill the morning would be well along. Adara didn't want the people there to find her vanished without a trace, so it was time for her to get home again. "You know, I think I might like to return to Carlienne for a visit," she told Ferdyn. "I've just about exhausted the adventuring prospects in Rivermarch, and I should go back to the Royal Library for some more study."

"You're welcome to stay here for as long as you like," Ferdyn told her softly. The way he said it, she knew he meant here, in his bed, back in his arms. Adara kissed him.

"This life is not for me," she said. "I love you, Ferdyn, but I'm not going to be your wife or your mistress. The world is full of people and places to discover, and I'm definitely not ready to settle down. Even when I do, I would probably rather do it the way my mother has, on a fine farm where there are meaningful tasks to engage in. But please say we can always be friends."

Ferdyn squeezed her tight, then released her and gave her a dirty grin. "With benefits?" he asked hopefully. Adara laughed, and kissed him again.

"With benefits," she replied.

# Chapter 3

Once again the family and household servants were clustered at the front entrance of Underhill to see Adara off. This time it was just her, with her two horses and Malika, who was leaving – Stellan having left on his own, mounted on Zoli, more than a week before.

"When are you coming back again?" Jaime asked hopefully. The boy seemed to have grown half a foot since they'd returned from their adventure at the end of last summer. An adventure on which he'd invited himself – that had earned him the love and respect of several members of the Karindas tribe of kobolds; a jewel-pommeled iridium short sword he practiced with every day; and months of being grounded with double chores. His parents had been convinced he must surely be dead by the time he'd returned to them, and their joy at the reunion had done little to allay their anger at the grief and worry he had caused them.

"I can't say for sure, it all depends on what I find when I get to Carlienne," his big sister said as she gave him a hug and a kiss goodbye. He might be nearly looking her in the eyes, the next time they met. She hadn't told the family about Fatiha Baba and its powers, fearing that if they knew she could return to them any time she liked they would expect her to be coming home for meals in the middle of her next adventure. She truly loved her mother and younger siblings, and had come to think fondly of her stepfather and many of the Underhill staff; but that didn't mean, at age eighteen, that she wanted to spend all her time with them.

So they expected that her trip to Carlienne, "to see old friends and visit the Royal Library," would require at least two weeks in either direction. After she had rounded the bend and the farm was no longer visible from the road she continued along the well-traveled but unpaved farm road in the direction of Willoughby for another mile. The early spring morning had started rainy, and the road was muddy.

They came to a crossroads, where the road from Underhill met the road that ran north to Willoughby and south over the hills to eventually come down, many miles away, at the outskirts of Riparre – capital of the duchy of Rivermarch. An enormous old oak tree stood watch over the intersection, and had sheltered many a traveler for an impromptu meal on the road during its long life. It also made an excellent landmark.

Adara had learned, after further experimentation with Fatiha Baba, that the imprisoned djinn could create a portal quite easily to anyplace it had done so for her before, without the need for her to form a detailed mental picture. It could also store impressions of places she had been while wearing the necklace, and thereafter be able to form portals to those places with only a brief mental reference.

"Fatiha Baba, this is the Willoughby crossroads," Adara told the djinn silently. She had begun wearing the enchanted necklace along with the Darkshield at all times, since it seemed that the ability to create a portal to a safe location might prove every bit as protective as the Darkshield's ability to ward off magic. They didn't go together very well stylistically, however. Fortunately, her daily life didn't often require her to accessorize.

"*I see, and remember,*" came the reply in her mind. Adara checked up and down the road, making sure no one was within sight. At this hour, and in this weather, the road was deserted. Next, she formed a picture of a spot along the road between Carlienne and King's Crossing, where last year she and Ferdyn had ridden together on several occasions. The Cooper family had been dazzled by Ferdyn's unexpected good fortune, and happy for him; but they had their own comfortable lives to lead, and still remained happily living in the small suburban town where Ferdyn and his brother had grown up.

This particular stretch of the road, around four miles beyond the northern outskirts of the capital, ran between broad farm fields. It was a major conduit for food coming into the city from the surrounding farms, but this early in the season there was little produce going to market. "Start with a small portal I can look through," Adara commanded the djinn. A little window in the air beneath the oak tree, maybe two feet on a side, appeared at a height of five feet from the ground.

Adara dismounted and stepped close to peer through. She stuck her head into the window, smelling the pre-dawn air, and looked up and down the road. As she'd hoped, nobody was stirring. "All right, take the portal down to ground level and make it big enough for me and the horses," Adara told her gatekeeper. By default, it seemed, the bottom edge of the portal was always at exactly the same height above the floor or ground at both ends. Since she was communicating mind to mind with the djinn, it was possible to fine-tune her requests precisely with no breakdowns in communication.

Malika had begun the journey perched on the front of Zarhya's saddle, but she had hopped down to the ground when they stopped. Go on through and wait, Adara sent silently to the semigryph. Without any hesitation she trotted over to the curious-looking dark rectangle and stuck her head in, sniffing. Then she did as she'd been bid. Adara mounted and urged Zarhya through the opening, Sadiq following calmly behind her on his lead line.

When the entire party had come through the opening and was well away from it, Adara had Fatiha Baba close it once again. The djinn had assured her that if a person or object was partway through a portal at the moment of closure, he, she, or it would merely be propelled unharmed to whichever side of the opening the majority of its mass was on at the moment – not gruesomely sliced in two, as she had imagined. But still...

By the time Adara and her animal companions reached the Palace District, the sun was coming up over the hills to the east. A much nicer morning here than in the area around Willoughby, it would seem. With its proximity to the sea, the capital's climate was mild. From up here one could see white sails dotting the bay that was spread out for miles to the south and east; and to the west, a bank of fog that obscured the view a mile or two offshore. On a clear day, from this highest point in the city, it was sometimes possible to glimpse the tallest peaks on the island kingdom of Elyrion, almost two hundred miles to the west.

Adara made her way to the King's Arms Inn, one of the capital's finest hostelries, and arranged for a room and stabling of the horses. A generous tip to the hostler assured that Malika would be allowed to sleep in the hay barn, helping to keep down the vermin. The two barn cats normally tasked with this duty gave her a wide berth, since she was more than double their weight and could fly.

It seemed odd to be checking into a hotel at this hour of the morning. Adara had already eaten breakfast with the family before leaving not two hours earlier, so she wasn't interested in a meal. After getting a couple of lads to drop her belongings in the spacious top-story room she'd rented, she wandered down to the common room and ordered a pot of tea.

It was possible that she could have stayed with Ferdyn, without him getting the idea that she had "come back to him." Their liaison a few mornings ago had been sweet, and she was looking forward to more in the future; but she preferred to keep a little distance between them. Who knew what opportunities might arise? And she didn't want to lead Ferdyn on, only to leave him in the lurch again when adventure called.

Adara pulled out a slim, leather-bound notebook she'd brought with her and began taking notes using a stick of graphite wrapped in cloth. She'd bought the book and begun recording her adventures after returning from the kobolds' lair last summer. Someday, she hoped to use her notes to produce some scholarly works on the ancient civilizations she'd re-discovered. But she lacked any formal education, having been schooled in reading, writing, and arithmetic (among more arcane subjects) only by Nanny Selden. Maybe she ought to hire a scholar, somebody who knew how these things were done, to ghost-write her memoirs instead.

She was dressed in a leather outfit she'd crafted herself, after paying Willoughby's armorer for lessons. He'd been dazzled at the speed with which the girl had learned what he had to teach, not knowing that the ring she wore on her left middle finger gave her the power to learn any skill, any knowledge with a fraction of the time and effort usually required.

As Adara sat sipping her tea and going through her notes, she caught the occasional inn patron eyeing her. *I do look pretty damn hot in this*, she thought. The long-sleeved jacket was made of tough but supple well-tanned cowhide, dyed black to match her raven locks, and worked with blued steel reinforcing the forearms, shoulder joints, and the area across her breasts. The shape of the breastplate perhaps *very slightly* overstated the size of those breasts, but not by much. After all, a girl had to breathe. The bottoms, skin-tight long pants with a double layer of leather on the seat and inner thighs, also had decoratively-worked blued steel plates providing extra protection in key areas.

With Voleur in its scabbard rising above her shoulder and her hair in a warrior's topknot, Adara resembled an elven warrior maiden from the ancient legends – or so she imagined. True, of the elves she'd met in her life so far only the merudur were taller than the average human – and she was a couple of inches short of how tall the average merudur woman stood. But she was nearly as slim and muscular.

Adara had many things to do while she was in Carlienne, but it was too early for most of them. However, smiths generally got an early start on the day. Downing the last of her pot of tea, Adara threw some coins on the tabletop and walked to the door. She would fetch Zarhya from the stables, and pay a visit to Falodar.

# Chapter 4

The elven smith Falodar had operated his smithy in Carlienne, not far from the waterfront, for more centuries than any of the Tanar capital's human residents could count. He was *the* elven smith in Carlienne, very nearly the only such anywhere within the kingdom since the Elvany War a couple of decades earlier.

Elyrion's attempt to wrest political control of the province of Elvany, a chunk of Tanar's southern coast within the duchy of Cornmarch, had led to disaster for the elves. The merudur king, Tersin, had seemingly seen himself as one of the ancient warrior-kings of the merudur come again – and he had rallied his people to fight for the right to control their one remaining stronghold on the continent of Eorla. The merudur were ship-builders, and some of the finest mariners on Q'ur; but the number of soldiers they could put in the field paled beside the legions of Tanar.

Yet Falodar had been supplying exquisitely crafted arms and armor to the human population of Tanar since not long after that kingdom had been unified, more than seven hundred years ago. King Tersin had been a stripling boy then, centuries away from the development of his political ambitions. And Falodar's elite human customers weren't going to let a little thing like the rise of anti-merudur sentiment in Carlienne prevent them from obtaining the finest weapons money could buy.

It was here that Adara had bought her irilium plate armor, custom-crafted to fit her body, last year before setting out on her journey back to Rivermarch. She liked the elven smith, an immensely tall fellow who as yet showed no signs of his centuries of life on his smooth, pale bluish skin. Had he been human, he might have been any age between thirty and fifty. As she guided Zarhya down Carlienne's stone-paved streets toward the Waterfront District, she mused on what it must be like to be a member of the udur. Kobolds, Siiri, pinudur, merudur, and all the rest grew old and died as did humans – but took twenty times as long doing it.

Despite Falodar's great age and prestige, Adara had not met with any underlings on her two previous visits to his shop. Normally a smithy would have at least a couple of apprentices, smithing being an ancient and much-valued trade. Perhaps the fact that the master was likely to last for several more centuries, instead of a few more decades, informed the elven notion of when it was time to ring in a successor. It also seemed to affect the quality of their work. No human smith had ever achieved such a degree of artistry. But that hadn't stopped the less-well-equipped humans from swarming over them on the field of battle.

Therefore Adara was brought to a halt, speechless, as she stepped inside the doors and found not Falodar but a clearly much-younger elf whaling away with hammer and tongs on what appeared to be an irilium breastplate. Such a piece, when completed, would be worth more than the hire of a skilled laborer for three years. And that meant this apprentice might actually be a journeyman. Irilium was supposedly the most difficult of all known metals to work, and the most valuable.

By Maridem, he was gorgeous! Adara had seen no more than a handful of merudur in her life, all of them here in Carlienne, and she had mostly found them a little too slender, a little too elongated – and a little too blue – for her taste.

The Siiri sorcerer Chtorias, whom she'd killed last year, had possessed the most beautiful features she had ever seen on a man – but she had overtopped him by three or four inches. This young smith (and by young, Adara supposed she meant a couple of centuries old) was nearly six and a half feet tall.

The air was warm inside the smithy and he was working shirtless, a heavy leather apron mostly protecting him from the heat and sparks of the forge. He was far more muscular than any merudur she had yet seen – not as hunky in proportion to his height as Ferdyn, certainly, but still far more powerfully built than his master Falodar. Furthermore his complexion, while pale, had a pinkish cast to it rather than the bluish tint of most merudur.

His face certainly looked elvish enough – somewhat elongated, beautifully sculpted features, no sign of facial hair, pointed ears, and eyes that were large and tilted up at the outside corners. His head hair appeared to be fine and nearly white, wrapped tightly in a knot atop his head to keep it out of his eyes as he worked.

Adara gaped, riveted by the beauty of the man before her as he concentrated on his work. It was poetry in motion, the flexing of the powerful arm and shoulder muscles as the hammer rose and fell, the concentration in the luminous eyes – which in the ruddy forge light looked dark purple. Unlike the Kier Ludzi, the merudur had eyebrows and eyelashes, which made them more attractive to human sensibilities.

She had momentarily forgotten why she was here, rendered speechless and paralyzed by the sight of this exemplar of elven manhood. He reached a point in the process of crafting the breastplate where he could take his attention away for a moment, and his own eyes went wide as he saw Adara – dilating to nearly black. His hammer strokes faltered, then he dragged himself back and resumed working – even as he spoke. "I'm sorry, can't stop now. Just another minute and I'll be with you."

The words were in Franca, perfectly fluent and with no trace of an accent. Fascinated, Adara continued drinking in the sight as the mysterious elven smith went on hammering, tapping, putting the breastplate over the heat again, taking it off. It was at least two minutes before he considered that it was now safe to down tools, and he set the nearly-completed breastplate into a sort of clay oven to the left of the forge. There, Adara guessed, it would stay at a temperature well above ambient until it was time to work on it some more.

The young paragon drew his forearm across his brow after setting down his tools, and stood gazing into Adara's eyes. His seemed to be purple one moment, blue the next. She was so rapt that it was he who finally broke the silence, by thrusting out his hand in a peculiarly human gesture. "Lemas Azarion at your service, lady," he said. Adara shook her head, trying to bring herself back to some semblance of awareness. What the fuck had just happened?

She took his hand. His grip was powerful, but he made no attempt to crush her hand. Nor did he bring it to his lips, as one of Carlienne's young bravos would surely have done. "Adara Willoughby," she said. "I, uh, have patronized Master Falodar in the past. I am hoping to speak with him about a commission."

Lemas smiled, and for an instant Adara found herself lost in those eyes again. "I took you for an elven maiden for a moment," he said. "Though no merudur e'er had such raven hair." His own hair, like that of most merudur, was as fine and silken as Adara's but pale in color.

"You're Falodar's apprentice?" Adara finally managed to stammer out. She still half felt as if she were floating on air. Lemas' grin seemed uncharacteristic for what little she knew of the merudur. Most of the udur races seemed very serious and full of themselves, disinclined for jollity with the inferior humans.

"And his grandson as well," he explained. "I am only recently come from Elyrion, but was apprenticed with a smith there for some years before coming to Carlienne."

Exerting the full force of her will, Adara brought herself back into focus. This was absurd! Most emphatically, she did *not* believe in love at first sight. Strong attraction at first sight, that might deepen into love after one actually got to know the person, sure. But in any case the idea of a love alliance with one of the udur was impossible. She'd be a faltering crone before this young elf had even gotten a glimpse of middle age.

That didn't stop the surge of lust she felt, looking at him standing there with his bare shoulders and arms, and that friendly expression on his beautiful face – way up there inches above her head. Might she just take an elven lover to see what it was like, knowing the relationship could not possibly go anywhere? At the moment, the temptation was strong. And it was distracting her from the reason she had come there.

Adara drew forth Voleur, and was pleased to note that Lemas did not flinch. It was unlikely that an elf as obviously young as he was could have seen combat, unless the clans in Elyrion were feuding with each other and she hadn't heard about it. But he seemed nonchalant about this martial-looking young woman drawing forth a serious blade.

"I like the weight, shape, and length of this blade," Adara told Lemas. "And I am interested in having a similar blade forged from irilium. I had occasion to bring this one to bear against the Belurii of the Siiri last year, and found that it fared poorly against irilium armor." Lemas' eyebrows, wing-like things darker by several shades than the hair on his head, rose in surprise.

18

"The Siiri?" he asked. "The aurudur? Surely they are long since vanished from Q'ur?" Adara gave him a wry smile.

"They decided to go into hiding underground," she told him. "And they built themselves one hell of a city down there. But they made the mistake, seven hundred years ago, of enslaving their fellow underground-dwellers the Kier Ludzi. That ended up not working out well for them."

Lemas gaped at her. He'd been struck by the beauty of this unexpected young woman. Now, he was seized by the desire to know everything about her. From her garb she was clearly an adventurer, and the way she moved suggested she was good at her trade. But she seemed so absurdly young! How was it possible?

"My grandfather is out on an errand, negotiating with ore suppliers along the docks," the apprentice smith told Adara. "He will not be back for probably another hour. Can I offer you some refreshment?" The kind of money the smithy's clients were willing to pay meant that they were treated with the utmost courtesy. And Lemas was happy to use that courtesy as an excuse to take an extended break.

Adara sheathed her blade and bowed slightly, smiling. Lemas felt a shiver run through him. He knew that liaisons with the daughters of men were doomed, but the desire for them was in his blood. Had his own heritage worked out differently, this Adara might have been an ideal mate. He led her back beyond the forge area, into the inner office, and seated her at the table where his grandfather usually conferred with customers.

Lemas brought out a bowl of roasted nuts, sweetened with honey, and a cool drink that tasted of flowers. Ambrosia, perhaps? Legends of Elyrion, the Blessed Isle, sometimes claimed that the merudur all spent their days lying around on satin cushions, partaking of such fare. It wasn't much to Adara's taste, but she politely accepted some. She was having a hard time keeping her eyes off her host.

"Please, Adara," he said, taking a seat across the table from her, "You must tell me everything about yourself." And she did, to some extent. Was there such a thing as magic that the Darkshield could not protect her from? In the course of half an hour, she had babbled far more about herself to this magnificent young elf than she had told Stellan in months of being his lover. What had come over her?

Finally Adara pulled herself up short. There were certain things she was determined not to reveal, at least not to someone she had just met. Ferdyn knew most of her secrets, but he was a trusted friend. "You've told me nothing about yourself, Lemas," she said at last. "Other than that you're Falodar's grandson, and an apprentice smith. What brought you to Carlienne from Elyrion?"

Lemas smiled ruefully. "I must be as honest with you as you have been with me, Adara," he said. "I sense that we will become good friends before long, and I would not hide the truth from you. There are some people in Elyrion who would prefer that I did not exist, and my father thought that it might be good for me to have a change of scene. Besides, my grandfather is regarded as one of finest smiths in Eorla, even among the merudur. It is an honor to be training with him."

Adara frowned. "There are people who would prefer you did not exist? What do you mean by that?" she asked. Lemas looked to be a fine specimen of the merudur race. And surely he was too young to have made any deadly enemies?

"I'm a half-breed," he explained. "My mother was a human woman, probably little older than you are now when I was born. But I was only a child when she died of old age."

So *that* explained his somewhat huskier build, his pinker complexion! Yet he looked the very picture of an elf. And if his mother had died of old age when he was a child, he had the long life to go with his looks. Lemas could tell from Adara's puzzled expression that she didn't understand, and he continued.

"You're aware that births among all races of the udur are far rarer than is the case among humans?" he asked, and Adara nodded. Even the brood mothers of the kobolds, far more fertile than any other udur females she knew of, only produced a child around every five years. "The seed of udur males is less copious than that of human males, but it is our women who are really at the heart of our lower fertility. Without that, I suppose we would long since have overrun the planet and stripped it of its resources, since our lifespans are so long."

Adara nodded, waiting for him to continue. She was learning something she had often wondered about. "When an udur male mates with a human woman, the chances of a child are not as great as if she had mated with a man of her own race. But they are still far greater than they would be had he mated with a woman of the udur. Yet of these children, three in four will usually be completely human. They will grow to adulthood in no more than twenty years, age and die in less than a century."

"And you're that fourth child?" Adara asked, beginning to see the picture.

"That's right," Lemas went on. "I got some of my physical appearance from my mother, it seems; but by and large I am of the merudur and can expect to live for many more centuries before I get old. Yet there are conservative factions among the merudur of Elyrion who talk about 'pollution of the race' and 'Elyrion for the purebloods.' They think it is a mortal sin for any of our people to breed with humans, or with other races of the udur such as the pinudur or caludur. And they discriminate against half-bloods like me, even though I am like they are – as well as against purebloods like my father, who took a human as consort."

Adara shook her head, musing. Considering there were plenty of humans who thought it was a sin and an abomination for the light-skinned humans of Eorla to intermarry with the dark-skinned people of Frigan, and that the merudur were famously convinced of their own superiority, she guessed they might find elf-human hybrids as disgusting as a cross between a human and some farmyard animal might be to the citizens of Tanar.

A thought occurred to her, and she asked "Did your mother and father have other children, Lemas?" He nodded. "I had a brother and a sister, both taller and more slender than our mother and paler of hair – but fully human. They both emigrated to Tanar when I was still a young child, after they had grown up. I have a pack of great-great-great and so forth grandnieces and nephews spread all over the continent, I guess. I don't actually know any of them."

How very odd, Adara thought, and rather sad as well. To love a person who was doomed to age and die before you had even finished growing up! "Your father remarried, then?" she asked. "The merudur

– so far as I know, the same is true for other races of the udur – do not marry as humans know it," Lemas explained. "Our lives go on for far too long, and it makes no sense to make a lifetime commitment. We take consorts, people who will live together in love with us for a time. And occasionally, it turns out to be a very long time. But every adult is expected to provide for themselves, and for the support and training of any children they may engender. There is no need for marriage to cement property rights."

"In any case," Lemas went on, "my father did take another consort – and rather quickly, since he had a half-grown son to raise. My stepmother gave birth to my little brother around twenty years later. That's unusual, as the conditions most likely to result in a pregnancy for a woman of the udur usually occur early in her relationship with her consort – often in the first year. It's probable that my presence interfered with her fertility. But she's happy enough now she has a son of her own, and I'm out of the house."

"You and she didn't hit it off?" Adara asked.

"It was fine when I was little," Lemas replied with a mournful note. "But after Dresan was born she no longer wanted to mother me. And by then I was in adolescence. I suppose even among humans, there can be conflicts when the children are at that stage." She raised her eyebrows.

"You might say that," she murmured with a half-smile.

An hour had flown by like nothing, and suddenly Falodar was there. He came through the forge, calling "Lemas? What…" then saw them sitting at the table. "I'd expected you to be working the forge," the master smith told his apprentice somewhat acerbically. He was of a height with his grandson, but of a much more wiry build. And his skin was pale, with the bluish tinge common to the merudur. Yet you could see the family resemblance.

"Sorry, Grandfather," Lemas said, rising to his feet. "Miss Willoughby came by to speak with you about a commission, and I couldn't keep her standing by the forge. I put the breastplate in the keeper box, so it will be all right for the time being."

Falodar looked from his grandson to the lovely young woman, a twinkle in his dark blue eyes. He held out a hand, "So good to see you again Adara. How's that armor working out for you?" She rose to take his hand, squeezing it warmly.

"It saved my life down in Zabran Lokaini last year, and several times since," she assured him. "I've already told Lemas all about my adventures, so I'll let you find out about them from him."

Adara drew Voleur, and laid it out on the table. "This is the first sword I ever owned," she told the smith and his apprentice. "I've come to find it a good size and design for me, but the steel blade is heavy and not hard and sharp enough to cut through iridium armor. I'd like to commission you to create a similar sword out of iridium, something with a good grip that will withstand the elements, and the same length as this."

Falodar eyed the blade thoughtfully. Though it was nothing fancy, he could see it was a fine weapon. He nodded. "Throw in some gems on the hilt and some runes incised in the blade, and you'd almost have the Sword of Myralis," he remarked. Lemas nodded too, but Adara drew a blank.

"The Sword of Myralis?" she asked, and Falodar smiled. "It was supposedly an enchanted merudur blade from the time of legends, some nine thousand years ago," he explained. Adara blinked. Nine thousand years was just a few long generations to the udur, she supposed. But back then her ancestors were only beginning to spread out in Eorla after supposedly coming here in dugout canoes from Frigan. They dressed in roughly tanned hides with the fur left on, and made their weapons out of stone or bronze.

"But the legends described the size and design of this sword?" Adara asked, surprised that not only a tale but descriptive details could have survived for so long.

"It's a legend specific to those of us in the smithing trade," Falodar explained. "Myralis was a warrior-queen of the merudur nation, back when we dominated this part of Eorla as well as the island of Elyrion. There's a whole lot of history about her, and I don't know it all. But her consort was Rohiran, a magus as well as the father of modern smithing. There was an epic song about him, how he came to discover the secrets of working in irilium, and how he crafted Prizal – Myralis' sword – and put enchantments on it so that she could use it lead the merudur to victory against the encroaching pinudur. It gave a very detailed description of the blade, right down to the gems and the rune-bespelled enchantments."

Adara's eyes had become dilated, and a siren song was whispering in her ears. Legendary treasure! Ancient mysteries! "So what became of this Prizal, then?" she asked casually.

"Lost," Falodar said with a shrug. "Queen Myralis led her troops to victory in the final battle against the pinudur, but she herself was killed near the end of it. The sword doesn't appear in any later legends, so I suppose it's probable they buried it with her. You might find something on it in the Royal Library, I suppose. After the recent war many volumes of elven history were brought from Meruzal and placed there. You might need someone to translate the material for you, though."

Most of the elves on the continent, at least those living above ground, could speak and write in Franca. But it was likely that ancient records from the time when the merudur ruled the lands that were now part of Tanar would have been in their own tongue. Adara had some ideas about that, though.

"Thank you, Falodar," Adara told the smith. "You've given me some food for thought. And Lemas, it was very good meeting you." They exchanged glances that raised the temperature in the room by a few degrees. "I'll be back in a day or two to see how you're coming along with the sword," she told them both. Then she sauntered out of the shop.

## Chapter 5

It was not yet noon, and she had snacked on those nuts at the smithy. But Adara decided to fortify herself with a bowl of excellent soup from the common room of the King's Arms after going up to her room and changing into more appropriate garb for a visit to the Royal Magus.

Cruztan Milegos, now well up in years, had been the Royal Magus to King Arden – and his father before him – for far longer than Adara had been alive. It had been he who guided her and Ferdyn to find and destroy the Mancer King, and in the months after they'd achieved that feat and returned to Carlienne in triumph she had consulted him often. Adara was only a little older than Julia, the old magus' great-granddaughter, who acted as a sort of personal secretary – and they had hit it off well.

So, she didn't bother visiting the Seneschal's office and working her way through the chain of middle-men to make an appointment. She just strolled into the magus' anteroom and greeted his young receptionist warmly. The girl, dark-haired and dark-eyed and beginning to fill out a little now at seventeen, jumped to her feet and came around the desk to take Adara by the hands and kiss her on the cheek. "Adara, you're back!" she crowed delightedly.

Adara threw her arms around the younger, shorter girl and gave her a hug. Julia was a sweetie once you got past her natural reserve, and quite bright as well. She'd acquitted herself well as her ancestor's assistant, and was now beginning to take lessons from him in the magical arts.

"I couldn't stay away," Adara told her. "I've missed you, and I've missed Sieur Milegos."

"What about Ferdyn?" Julia asked. She had thought Adara's relationship with the handsome, dashing adventurer romantic in the extreme when she'd first met the pair last year, and it had saddened her to learn that they'd split up. Of course, he *was* awfully old. Almost thirty!

"Ferdyn and I are still friends," Adara assured her with a smile. "But just friends. It wasn't going to work out between us, with him liking the urban high life and me preferring to be out in the hinterlands exploring dusty ruins." There was little sign that she had ever performed such activities, dressed as she was in a sober-looking and fabulously expensive silk gown.

"Oh, you must tell me all about your adventures!" Julia insisted.

"And so I shall," Adara promised. "And the magus as well. Is he free at the moment?" The old Royal Magus was rarely called upon to perform much magic these days, but despite his advanced age he was still hale and hearty. He spent most of his time in study and experimentation.

Julia twinkled. "I think he's been reading some tomes I dragged up from the Royal Library since right after breakfast," she said. "I'm sure he'd be glad to take a break. Have you eaten?" Everybody she met today seemed to want to feed her, Adara mused.

"I had some soup a little while ago, but I wouldn't mind something light," she allowed. Julia stepped out into the corridor and flagged down a passing page. "Bring a plate of fruit and sandwiches to the Royal Magus' quarters, enough for three," she commanded with the authority of one born not to the nobility but to a lifetime of privilege. The boy hurried off to do her bidding.

Next, Julia led the way through to the quarters where Cruztan spent most of his working hours – a large chamber littered with intriguing artifacts. "Papí, look who's here!" she called out to the old man seated at a writing desk with a thick and ancient-looking book spread out on its polished wooden surface.

Milegos looked up and his dark eyes lit at the sight of Adara. He had adopted her as an unofficial descendant, it seemed. He rose to his feet without the slightest trace of infirmity and strode toward her, arms out. "I'd feared we had seen the last of you, my dear!" he exclaimed, enveloping her in an avuncular hug.

"Nobody's gotten the better of me yet, thanks in large part to your help, old one," Adara said cheerfully. Soon the three of them were clustered around the table where last year she had first shown the old magus the Darkshield, and learned of its properties. On that occasion he had given her the enchanted ring she called her "Learning Ring." It had allowed her to acquire skills beyond what anyone her age might be expected to have, and those skills had saved her bacon on more than one occasion.

Soon the refreshments arrived, and Adara nibbled on a couple of finger sandwiches and some fruit, washed down with spring water, as she told the old man and his young assistant all that had transpired since her last visit with them. As Ferdyn had often gotten short shrift in the tales of her adventures she'd related since then, poor Stellan was now relegated to a footnote. The hot passion they'd shared was nothing an octogenarian and his (presumed) virginal great-granddaughter needed to hear about.

As she thought about it, it occurred to Adara that she seemed to have gotten over feeling bad about Stellan's departure. Ever since her pre-dawn visit with Ferdyn, and just today being thunderstruck with desire at meeting Lemas, she no longer had any trace of regret. She was young; and there were many, many fish in the sea.

The tales and the meal wound up at about the same time, and Cruztan asked, "So, how is it you have returned to us, Adara? Do you have a line on a new historical mystery to explore?" She gave him a secret smile. He knew her too well.

"Today I was talking with Falodar, the merudur smith," she began. Milegos nodded. He knew the man of old. For a human interested in history, it only made sense to cultivate the acquaintance of as many of the udur as possible. Only from them could you get first-hand accounts of events that had happened hundreds or thousands of years in the past.

"He was speaking of an artifact known as Prizal, the Sword of Myralis," Adara went on. "Supposedly it was buried with the elven queen who bore it, and I was hoping to find some more information in the Royal Library. He mentioned that after the Elvany War a lot of merudur books were confiscated from the library at Meruzal."

Adara sat back on the comfortably-upholstered settee and watched the magus' brilliant mind go to work. He was almost a walking Royal Library himself, having spent decades researching dozens of different subjects. After almost a full minute he spoke. "Myralis," he said. "An iconic figure in merudur legend. She was the first of the warrior-rulers of that people, thousands of years ago when the human population of Eorla was still far smaller than that of the elves who had dominated the continent since pre-history."

His audience, both Adara and Julia, sat forward – eager to hear more. Julia's decision to work closely with her great-grandfather had not been mere chance. Of all his many descendants, it was she who shared his bent for magic – and for scholarly pursuits.

"You must understand," the old man went on, "the merudur have always existed as a nation as much as a race. So it usually is with the udur, though there are always individuals who break away and go where they please. At the time of Myralis, the merudur nation controlled nearly all of present-day Tanar west of the Ratskells and south of the Neigandes, all the way south to the Surden Sea – as well as the island of Elyrion, which so far as anyone knows they have always occupied."

Adara hadn't realized this, but then they were talking about times many thousands of years in the past. The way things had been then hardly seemed relevant to the modern world, but as she thought about it she realized that from the perspective of the merudur that time frame equated to less time ago than the Unification of Tanar. Humans might think such times too distant to worry about, but they shared the world with people who didn't hold that view. It was a pity that only the children of the wealthy were ever given any instruction in history!

"In any case," Cruztan went on, "the merudur were hard-pressed by the pinudur who controlled most of what we now call Nordstan. Considering the climate up there, it should not be a surprise that they hoped to expand their dominion south into the lands with a longer growing season. But the merudur were determined to resist. Of course, millennia after they successfully drove back their fellow elves, they were ousted from the continent by humans. But that's another tale."

Adara and Julia both nodded, and the old magus continued. "It was said that after the defeat of the pinudur the merudur went into a long period of peace and prosperity – long for them, and that's far longer than the kingdom of Tanar has existed. But I haven't read any details of that, nor much mention of this Prizal you spoke of, save that Queen Myralis wielded it and it gave her absolute dominion over her enemies. Despite that, she was among those slain in that final battle. I haven't had the opportunity to look over the materials brought from Meruzal, of course."

"Are you able to read the old merudur writings?" Adara asked, and Cruztan nodded.

"I learned their runes many years ago," he said. "I had originally wanted to be a scholar, and only came to magic as a side effect of my studies."

"Can you teach me?" Adara asked, giving him her best blue-eyed, hopeful gaze. The old mage looked back at her thoughtfully. Then he nodded again.

# Chapter 6

Celine Biston blinked as she opened the door to see a tall, slim young woman in a finely-tailored silk dress standing on the mat. At her side was a creature that somewhat resembled a huskily-built, oversized housecat. Sitting, it came up to her knees. And were those *wings* folded at its sides? It eyed her with a calm golden gaze, as Adara said "Madame Biston, remember me? Adara?"

The middle-aged housekeeper started back. She had barely begun working here, the better part of a year ago, when the young woman cohabiting with her master had pulled up stakes and moved on. Since then there had been a veritable parade of lovely young women through the house, so many that Celine had long since lost count. But far be it from her to pass judgment on the young master and his doings. Was he not one of the quality?

After looking Adara up and down, Celine sniffed almost inaudibly. "You're here to see Master Ferdyn, I assume?" Oh, so it was like *that*, was it? Since she'd begun hobnobbing with the nobility, it had always struck Adara as strange that those whom they hired to serve them could be twice as snobbish as they were themselves. She raised her chin, looking down on Ferdyn's housekeeper and chief servant from her advantage of five inches of extra height.

"See me in at once," she snapped, without any explanation of the reason for her visit – or the strange animal companion at her side.

Madame Biston ceded the field, and Adara and Malika were ushered into the downstairs parlor. The townhouse was three stories, each more elegant than the last, and most of the ground floor was devoted to spaces where the occupants might entertain. No more than a couple of minutes after Adara had been seated, Ferdyn came bounding downstairs from the floor above and swept her into his arms. "You made it!" he declared, with obvious pleasure, and she smilingly embraced him.

Ferdyn might indeed not qualify as the love of her life, and Adara's experience with Lemas this morning had shaken her; but she had to admit that being in his presence filled her with warmth. He was just so damned... likeable. And sexy as hell, of course. She'd learned a few things since his tutelage in the arts of love, but as her first he would always hold a special place in her sexual memories.

They might have agreed to be friends – with benefits – but Ferdyn's embrace left no doubt that those benefits were much on his mind. From the way his hands squeezed her buttocks through the thin fabric of her dress, to the firmness she could feel in his well-tailored trousers, his desire was evident. And contagious.

Adara pushed him away after a minute, as it seemed he might intend to ravish her right here in the parlor. Panting slightly, she gestured toward the semigryph. "I thought you might like to meet Malika," she said. The fact that she'd acquired a semi-sentient animal companion on her way back to Rivermarch last year had been mentioned but briefly. He gazed into her eyes, and Adara felt an electric thrill from the heat that was conveyed. Then he looked down at Malika, and melted.

"Gods, an actual tame semigryph," he murmured, and dropped to one knee. "Can I pet her?" he asked, looking up at Adara for reassurance. She queried the semigryph mentally; but like everyone else Ferdyn met, it seemed, she had already been won over.

"Scratch her behind the ears, she really likes that," Adara suggested.

Blessed Maridem, the man had gone completely over the edge. He was scratching Malika behind both ears at once, running his hands along the fur of her back, and crooning "Who's a pretty girl, then? You are! Oh yes, you are!" Adara realized she had never seen Ferdyn in the presence of a pet animal before. They kept no pets, not even a barn cat, at the Cooper residence in King's Crossing. Why had he not gotten one during the nearly a year since he'd bought this place, if he was this crazy about animals? Or perhaps, had he? She had only been here once before this year, and the subject of pets had not come up.

Malika radiated delight at Ferdyn's over-the-top devotion, as Adara just stood bemused, taking in the scene. Amazing how you could think you knew someone, and then… She still felt she had never really known Stellan, and wondered what he was thinking and doing at this moment. Quickly, the wistful thought was banished from her mind.

Finally Ferdyn rose to his feet again and beckoned to Malika to hop up onto the couch. Then he sat beside her and ran his hand along the silken fur of her back. She let out a deep purr, and appeared to fall asleep. He was grinning from ear to ear, drawing Adara in against her will. She sat on the settee opposite and smiled. "I've never seen her hit it off so well with someone who wasn't giving her food," she remarked, and he grinned.

"She's absolutely beautiful!" he said enthusiastically. "And you said you can communicate with her mentally?" Adara nodded.

"It's an extension of the same mental techniques I use for riding," she explained. "Malika doesn't have words, but since she was just a half-drowned kit with a broken wing I've been able to exchange emotions and concepts with her. And with Fatiha Baba, I can actually carry on telepathic conversations."

"I'm in awe of your skills," Ferdyn assured her. "So, how long have you been in town?" Adara filled him in on the activities of the day, of course omitting the thunderbolt of attraction that had blossomed between her and the young elven smith. She still hadn't figured out what, if anything, to do about that. Sure, she could hop into bed with him. But then what? Better if she could just put Lemas out of her mind.

Ferdyn, unaware that he was doing so, was happy to help. It turned out that he had no social activities planned for the evening. Adara wondered if he might have been saving his time for her, knowing that she would soon be arriving in Carlienne. They had an intimate supper in the second-floor family dining room, feasting on shrimp, scallops, fish, and lobster from Carlienne Bay in a sauce rich with cream, butter, garlic, and lemon. This was served over thin noodles with a side of seasonal greens, and was so delicious Adara had seconds. Malika got a share as well, and pronounced it wonderful.

After supper the two of them went to a second-floor parlor to sit side-by-side on a comfortably-upholstered love seat. Malika squeezed in beside Ferdyn, and soon dropped off to sleep. He put his arm around Adara, and gazed down at her with an expression of warm affection. "I can't tell you how good it is to have you here," he said softly. He was working hard to keep it light, but she had a glimpse of the hurt he had felt when she'd left him. The hurt he might never truly get over.

"I love being with you, Ferdyn," Adara told him truthfully. "You are one of the sweetest people I know. I'm sorry that it didn't work out between us, but I hope I'll always have your friendship. Even after we're both old and married to someone else." A shadow crossed his cheerful features so briefly she might almost have missed it, had she not been paying close attention.

With a soft growl, Ferdyn took Adara in his arms and locked his mouth on hers. Their clinch quickly progressed to stroking, groping, and heavy breathing. Her breasts came free from the top of her dress, and Malika – disturbed by all the activity – got up with a sniff and went over to sleep on a quieter couch. Minutes later Adara's skirts were up around her waist, her underdrawers sliding down past her knees. As Ferdyn's hot, hard cock found her slit and began working its way inside, she closed her eyes. And thought of Lemas.

# Chapter 7

During the next week Adara spent most of her time at the palace, taking lessons in Old Merudur from Cruztan Milegos. Fortunately the ancient elvish runes were an alphabetic system akin to what humans in Eorla had adopted. Perhaps, their system had even been copied or adapted from what the once-rulers of the continent had used. In any case, they were phonetic representations of the merudur tongue. It took her less than a day to learn the runes and the sounds they represented. All the rest of that time was spent learning the language itself.

As the tongue was spoken by the old magus, Adara could detect a fluidity that reminded her of the tongue of the Siiri. Were the two languages related? She discussed it with Cruztan, and he was convinced that the tongue of the aurudur and that of the merudur were both descended from an Ur-udur, a language used by the ancestral elves before whatever event had caused Q'ur's first sentients to split into many different races.

Adara doubted it would be possible to prove or disprove Cruztan's theory, so many millennia down the road – and given that the udur, by and large, were insular people who were disinclined to let themselves be studied by short-lived, upstart humans. But she was able to supply a lot of information about the Kier Ludzi, which he found fascinating.

The striking biological differences between the kobolds and other elves, coupled with the fact that they themselves acknowledged that they *were* elves, only gave them a new mystery to ponder. Adara wondered if it would ever be resolved.

Outside the time spent in lessons and study, Adara found herself visiting Falodar's smithy a lot. Her excuse was that both the smith and his apprentice were native speakers of Merudur, albeit the modern tongue and not its archaic antecedent as recorded in the records taken from Meruzal. Since she was only trying to understand what had been written down thousands of years ago, it didn't really make sense for her to be trying to improve her pronunciation. She didn't care.

She had declined to spend that first night in Ferdyn's bed. After the second time they'd made love that night, she had used Malika as a lame excuse to flee back to the King's Arms. He'd clearly been disappointed, but Adara couldn't let him begin to think she had come back to him. She loved him, she wanted him – and she was not ever going to belong to him. Only one more time during the week had she agreed to come to his house, and again the sex had been epic – and meaningless. Adara felt as though she was dissolving inside, torn into tiny pieces by her conflicting desires. She needed to get away.

On the seventh day, as evening was coming on, Adara arrived at Falodar's smithy with Malika by her side. She'd been leaving the semigryph behind during her long sessions at the palace, but liked to take her animal companion with her when she could. The pair of them had provoked much comment, though Malika had mostly kept her feet on the ground during their excursions. She'd discovered early on that the pigeons swarming around Carlienne were beyond her skill to catch.

Lemas had been tidying up around the forge, preparing to shut down for the day, and his beautiful face lit as he saw them come into the shop. "Wait'll you see!" he said excitedly, "It's absolutely spectacular!" Falodar was no magus, and unable to duplicate the enchantments that had been laid on Prizal; but he had easily talked Adara into allowing her new sword to be decorated with similar gems.

Money was no object, for her; and she'd been taken by the old smith's enthusiasm. He seemed to feel as though her commission was an opportunity for him to channel the legendary figure who'd been the father of his craft. The sword he was making for Adara was not just a weapon – it was Falodar's most significant work of art in centuries.

And yet, it had taken him – and Lemas – only a week to create. Adara doubted that either of them had worked on anything else, during all the hours she'd spent mastering the tongue of the ancient merudur. It gave her a little thrill to have been the instigator of this creative effort. Sure, the millions in gold she'd stolen from the Mancer King's storehouse had made it all possible – but she didn't think for a moment that the smiths, master and apprentice, had only done it for money.

Lemas reached down to stroke Malika's head as Adara and her furry companion came in through the forge area to the office. He was not nearly so besotted with the semigryph as Ferdyn, but he had still come to like the little creature – and she was at least tolerant of him.

For a member of a famously shy and stand-offish species, Malika seemed remarkably happy to welcome new admirers whenever she found them. Adara assumed that the mental bond she'd established with her when the semigryph was only half grown had affected her outlook as a near-adult. It remained to be seen what would happen when she reached sexual maturity.

Lemas ushered them into the office, where the new sword lay – sitting on a piece of black velvet fabric – atop the table. It glimmered in the lamplight, the flickering of flames reflecting in its polished irilium surfaces, the small gems that had been set into the hilt to provide a gripping surface, the large faceted ruby that formed the pommel. Adara's breath caught in her throat as she stared at it, scarcely believing this exquisite object was hers – and that she intended to use it to kill people with. How could she possibly?

Lemas, behind her, took her by the shoulders and squeezed gently, gazing at the sword as they shared the moment. Adara wondered whether he, whether any other smiths, ever experienced the emotional disconnect she had just discovered – between the beauty of the weapons they crafted and the ugliness, the finality, of the death those weapons could bring. She shuddered slightly, and Lemas put his long, strong arms around her and hugged her to his chest.

He laid his smooth cheek alongside hers and murmured in her ear, "Have you thought of a name for her?" Her? Though Ferdyn had named his sword Virago and had always referred to it as "her," Adara had named her own salvaged sword for the thief she'd taken it from and thought of it, when she put such thoughts into words, as "it." It was an inanimate object, a thing of stark utilitarian beauty. But this…!

Despite her ambivalence, repelled by the sword's purpose as she was drawn to its beauty, Adara knew that this thing she had caused to be created must have a name. And as it was, in some way, the descendant of Myralis' ancient blade, its name must be in the ancient tongue of the merudur. "Sierlas," she said softly. Then louder, "Her name is Sierlas." Judgment.

Lemas gave her shoulders another squeeze, then nodded. He had never killed anyone with the weapons he made, but this incredibly young woman who filled him with such hopeless longings had. Adara abruptly came to a decision. This close to Lemas, she could smell his sweat – and while it was not a rank odor, it was distracting.

"You live here at the smithy?" she asked, turning to face Lemas and looking up into his eyes. The building pre-dated much of the city of Carlienne, and there was a broad second story above the forge and office. He nodded, puzzled. They had talked of many things during her visits over the past week, but that subject had not come up.

"And do you have a bathroom here?" Adara asked next. Lemas' pale complexion flushed pink. He had gotten too close to her, and he stank! She must be repelled.

"We just use a basin to wash up in, most days," he admitted. "When this place was built, I don't think bathrooms had been invented yet. The privy is out back."

She smiled at him, relieving his fears. "I'd like to invite you to dine with me at my inn this evening," Adara explained. "The King's Arms in the Palace District. Do you know it?" Since arriving in Carlienne only a few months ago, the young elf had had little reason to visit the Palace District.

"I know how to find the district," he said. "And I suppose I can ask directions once I get there."

"It's only a few blocks down Queen Miranda Street from the east entrance to the palace grounds," she told him. "A three-story building with a large sign on two sides picturing the Ruicine family crest. You can't miss it. But I think it would be a good idea if you could get a hot bath first. The place is pretty fancy."

Lemas blushed again, head lowered. While smithing was the most honorable of trades, a smith was still a laborer – someone who worked with his hands. In Tanar, much more so than in Elyrion, such people were never admitted to the highest echelons of society. But – a chance to dine with Adara, away from the eyes of his grandfather!

"I'll go to the public bathhouse," he told her, recovering from his embarrassment. "What time should I be at the inn?" The smithy possessed a beautiful clock of pinudur manufacture, which sat in a position of pride atop the mantle in the room they were standing in. It was now a little past five.

"Shall we say seven?" Adara asked, picking up Sierlas and slipping her into the sheath on her back. She fit perfectly, a gem glittering atop the plain setting of the sheath that had been made for Voleur.

"See you at seven then," Lemas said, joy shining in his deep violet eyes. Adara smiled up at him, then stood on tiptoe and planted a kiss on his cheek. To her astonishment, the tall young elf flushed crimson.

# Chapter 8

Adara sat at the small table she'd commandeered in the King's Arms inn's spacious and well-lit common room, nursing a glass of wine and looking around her anxiously. What was keeping him? From the look in Lemas' eyes when she'd invited him to join her this evening, she had half expected him to be here half an hour early even if he *did* have to go bathe first. What time was it, anyway?

The door at the far end of the room opened, and there he stood – looking magnificent! He was scrubbed and dressed in a blue linen tunic and green leggings, soft low boots on his feet and a worried expression on his face. If Lemas had experienced prejudice in his native land for his half-blood heritage, here in Carlienne he would be seen as a full elf – and many yet lived who were veterans of the Elvany War. It was perfectly reasonable for him to enter this upscale inn with trepidation, though he was more likely to be assaulted in the low dives near Falodar's smithy.

Adara had a moment of doubt. Had it been wise to expose him – and herself – to unfriendly eyes? Maybe she should have invited him out on a picnic. Well, too late now. She got to her feet and waved at Lemas, but he'd already spotted her and was making his way toward the table. He stood at least three inches taller than anyone else in the room, his pale silken hair freshly washed and brushed and hanging over his shoulders and halfway down his back. He was so beautiful it took her breath away.

As he came up to the table he took Adara in from head to toe with an expression of awe and delight, making her feel well-rewarded for the effort she'd put into her appearance this evening. She too was freshly bathed, and she'd donned one of the sexier gowns in her wardrobe. She'd left quite a few such in a spare closet at Ferdyn's, and had retrieved some of them on her last visit. He hadn't asked her why.

Adara sat down, and Lemas took the seat opposite her – still devouring her with his eyes. "You were right," he said, "this place was easy to find. It's the first inn I've been to since I got to Carlienne that wasn't on the waterfront." He looked around him with a shy smile. "Nice place," he added. The other patrons were wealthy merchants for the most part, and if some of them eyed the tall elf surreptitiously and wondered what he was doing here, nobody was rude about it.

Adara flagged a barmaid. "We're ready to order now," she said. The girl curtsied, and pulled out a notepad.

"We have the roast beef with cabbage and potatoes, or the fried filet of flounder with spring greens and fried potatoes," she said. Other dishes were available here, at one of the capital's finest hostelries, but these were the specials.

Feeling like a bumpkin and trying hard not to show it, Lemas told Adara "I'd prefer the beef. As you can imagine, we eat a lot of fish in Elyrion." The barmaid's eyes grew wide at the comment. Here was a genuine elf, from the mystic island kingdom of Elyrion! She'd never seen one close up before, and was astonished at how muscular and handsome he was.

Adara smiled, and said "I'll have the same. I've been lunching at the palace all week and they've been serving a lot of fish there, as well."

The girl jotted down their orders. "And bring us a bottle of the '76 de Grenvale, if you would," Adara added. Two years ago she wouldn't have known a de Grenvale red from one of the tart products of the Cornmarch vintners; but her time in Carlienne last year, helped along by her Learning Ring, had greatly improved the sophistication of her palate.

Lemas raised his eyebrows. From her appearance Adara could not be much more than twenty, yet she had done so much and seemed so confident and sophisticated. He was ten times her age, and felt at sea in this situation she commanded so easily.

As they waited for the food to arrive, they engaged in light conversation. "I think you'll like the de Grenvale," Adara said smoothly. "I actually rescued Chateau de Grenvale from being burned to the ground about a year ago, which was when I first got the chance to taste their wines. The viscount and his lady were very nice, and quite grateful."

"I can't believe how many adventures you've had, Adara," Lemas replied. "How old are you, really?"

"I just turned eighteen in Warming," she said, "but I've been considered an adult for the past two years. Most of the girls my age back home in Pine Hill are already married with children." A wing-like brow shot up as he took this in. At the age of eighteen, he'd been out of diapers – but still only a fraction of his adult height.

"What about you, Lemas?" Adara asked. "Or should I call you 'old one'?" The discrepancy in their lifespans was at the crux of her reluctance to get involved with the young elf. Even if they were at similar places in their lives, there could not be a long-term relationship for them. At least not from his perspective. But she wanted him, badly!

He colored. "I'm two hundred five, two hundred six next autumn," Lemas admitted. "The merudur consider age two hundred to be legal adulthood. At that age you are allowed to sign contracts, take consorts, and control any property you've inherited. But in terms of how society regards people my age, I think I'm a little younger than you are."

*That* explained it! Adara had wondered at how shy and hesitant Lemas seemed. He must have led a pretty sheltered existence for those two centuries. Wait a second… "Did you say you can't take a consort until you're two hundred?" Adara asked. Lemas blushed again, and hung his head.

"That's right," he mumbled. "A lot of adolescents fool around with sex, but you're not expected to set up housekeeping with a lover until you're of age. You have to remember that raising an elven child is a long-term commitment. Though unintended pregnancies aren't something that happens a lot."

Adara fixed him with a blue-eyed stare. "And you, Lemas? Did you 'fool around' with sex when you were an adolescent?" He gazed down at the tabletop, then into her eyes.

"No," he mumbled shortly. "I've never had the opportunity. Not too many families would want one of my kind getting friendly with their daughters."

Maridem save me, Adara thought. This was going to be interesting! "So you haven't ever…?" Eyes on the tabletop again.

"No." Just then he was saved from further embarrassment by the arrival of their meals, fine china plates heaped high with juicy slabs of roast beef, boiled potatoes, and cabbage. Not the fanciest of fare, but this was after all an inn – not the royal palace.

Lemas seized knife and fork and eagerly attacked his supper, washing it down with frequent drafts of the red wine Adara had ordered. He had to admit, it was delicious. The cool maritime climate of Elyrion produced wines that were light, and usually pretty dry.

Adara tucked into her own food, watching Lemas with some astonishment. Gods, how the boy could eat! Now that she knew how his age compared with her own, and the fact that he was a virgin, she could not help thinking of him as a boy – even if he overtopped her by eight inches and could probably pick her up with one hand.

Gee, I seem to be working my way toward younger and younger men, Adara thought as he chewed the succulent red meat. Which was absurd, considering the earliest ancestors she knew about hadn't been born yet by the time Lemas got out of diapers. But both Ferdyn and Stellan had possessed a wealth of life experience she could learn from. Now, it seemed, she would become the teacher.

The meal was done, and the second bottle of wine was down to the last half a cup. Both Adara and Lemas were feeling replete, warmed, and relaxed. But at the back of Adara's mind there was a faint tension, a tingling. She'd planned this evening before realizing what she was taking on. Was she up to it? Hell yes, but first let the food slide down a little.

They sat talking for another hour, avoiding the earlier subject entirely. Then Adara got to her feet. "Follow me," she said, with a beckoning gesture. Lemas gulped, rose to his feet, and trailed behind her as she led the way to the staircase leading up to the inn's rooms on the second and third floors. The evening was yet young, the common room was doing a roaring business in drinks, and nobody much noticed them as they slipped through the crowd and vanished up the stairs.

Adara's room was the largest and most opulently appointed of the rooms on the third floor, which went at a premium because of their views and the fact that the noise of the common room didn't penetrate this far. Lemas was trailing behind her like a porter, not walking with his arm around her like a man who expected to be climbing into her bed in the near future. The poor boy, he probably had no idea *what* to expect. She noted that when the subject of sexual experience had come up, he had *not* similarly quizzed her. Perhaps her remark that most girls her age were married mothers had led him to assume that Adara had more experience in that area than he did.

Adara pulled the room key from a velvet drawstring pouch at her waist, and let them both into the room. She'd left an oil lamp burning earlier, and a warm glow greeted them as they stepped inside. The bed was huge, half again as large as a normal "double" bed, and bore a puffy feather mattress. Plus there was a sitting area with a table and chairs, a small couch, and even a privy chamber tucked behind a screen in the corner. In daylight, the windows offered a view of Carlienne Bay.

"Wow, this place is something," Lemas said as he stood just inside the door looking around. His own quarters above the smithy, as utilitarian as Falodar's own, were clean and in good repair. That was about all you could say for them. The home he'd grown up in, near the southeastern tip of Elyrion, was considerably more elegant. But even its amenities were not the equal of these.

"I'm glad you like it," Adara purred. She had unexpectedly found herself cast as the older woman, the seductress, and it was a role she had no prior experience with. She only knew she wanted this young man badly, was in love or more likely in lust with him – and hang the consequences. It was hard to imagine a more ill-considered match, and she didn't care.

Adara motioned for Lemas to join her on the small couch, roughly the same size as the one on which she and Ferdyn had made love a few nights ago. It was clear he was nervous, and getting more so. She took his hands. There had been very little actual physical contact between them since they had met, though their eyes had said much. She looked into his now, like pools of night in the dim light.

"Lemas," Adara said gently, "I think it's time you learned about the ways of a man with a woman." He blinked, and squeezed her hands. He was eager, so eager, for what she was offering him. And half-terrified, as well. "I know," she went on, "that our differing lifespans mean we can't have a life together. I can't, should not, be your consort and I don't intend to bear your children. But I like you, and I want you. Can you accept that?"

He nodded, and licked his lips anxiously. What next? Adara leaned forward and pressed her lips to his. He almost pulled back, but as the sensations grew he suddenly wanted more, wanted to lose himself in her mouth, in her body. He kept his lips closed, though; and in a few moments Adara pulled away.

"That was nice," she said, "but it would be nicer like this…" She pressed herself to him, and as their lips met her mouth opened and her tongue slipped between his lips. It was as if an electric shock had surged through him. His member went rock-hard in an instant, tightly confined within his codpiece, and he let his own tongue move forward and into Adara's mouth. Though they had both had the same thing for dinner, and drunk the same wine, her mouth somehow tasted sweet to him.

They broke apart, panting. Lemas' eyes were wide, and he was seized with the desire to ravish Adara on the spot. If he had any idea how to go about doing that… Since he did not, he decided it would be best to wait on her instruction. He had the feeling he was going to enjoy it, and he trusted her completely.

Adara gazed into his eyes, her own dilated with desire. There was something so… inflaming, about being with an utterly gorgeous man who did not yet have a clue. Her dress had been artfully tailored to make the most of her smallish but high and firmly rounded breasts. She gestured toward them. "Put your hands on me, Lemas," she commanded, and he obeyed.

With the slightest of shrugging gestures, Adara let the dress slide down off her shoulders – releasing her breasts so that they were fully exposed for Lemas' enjoyment. She wondered idly how many years it was that elven mothers nursed their babes, as without any prompting whatsoever his right hand went around the left one as his mouth sought the right.

Adara gasped and shuddered. "Yes," she sighed, "that's good. Keep doing that, gently." She reached down and lifted the hem of her dress up around her hips, exposing her thighs. Lemas was busy, but he noticed with a start that she was not wearing any underdrawers. He had never even seen the naked crotch of an adult woman before, and he was so fascinated that it tore his attention away from what he was doing. He watched as Adara, knees apart, ran her hands up her thighs and into the neatly-trimmed bush of raven hair at her cleft. She spread her labia so he could get a good look at the goal, and breathed, "Come closer…"

Her lovely silk dress balled up around her waist like a sash while her breasts and lower body were exposed, Adara leaned back on a cushion with her knees up and her legs spread. Lemas, a jolt of excitement running through him, leaned closer for a good look. Adara used a forefinger to prod her clit, which was swollen and throbbing. "That's my clitoris," she told her eager pupil. "It's sort of the same kind of thing as a man's penis, and it feels really good to stimulate it. But the little tip is super sensitive. It's better not to touch that part, but just to rub and press on the flesh surrounding it. Feel!"

Fascinated, Lemas brought his hand with its long, graceful yet powerful fingers down between her legs. "It's stiff, like my penis," he said wonderingly. "And the little opening right below?"

"That's my urethra, where urine comes out," his instructress said clinically. "But the bigger opening below there, inside the lips, is my vagina. That's where we'll be going in a moment."

Lemas might be a 205-year-old virgin, but his instincts seemed to be good. He bent between Adara's legs to plant a sweet kiss on her vulva. The clean scent, the taste of it inspired him to run his tongue along, from her vaginal opening up across the vestibule to the underside of her clit. Adara moaned, and put both hands on his head. "Oh, that feels good!" she breathed. "Do that some more!" So excited was Adara, after having wanted to jump Lemas' bones for most of the past week, that even his neophyte efforts at cunnilingus were enough to carry her off.

She bucked, muscles spasming, and Lemas tasted a slightly salty fluid. Her entire vulva was reddened and glistening, seeming swollen in the dim lamplight. He raised his head to look her in the eyes, pleased with himself. "You liked that?" he asked, with innocence so sweet Adara had to laugh.

"Yes, that was very nice," she said encouragingly. "Come on, let's get rid of these clothes, shall we?"

Adara got to her feet and wriggled out of her dress, scooping it up off the floor and giving it a shake before hanging it on one of the hooks the King's Arms management had provided. Dresses of this caliber were not to be trampled underfoot!

Meanwhile Lemas had peeled off his tunic, and stood revealed naked to the waist in all his smooth-skinned, muscular glory. He was gaping at Adara, drinking in her long legs and lean curves. "Are you sure you're not part elf?" he asked. The women of the merudur were almost all Adara's shape, tall and slender. She might not be every human male's ideal woman, but to him she was stunningly beautiful.

She grinned at him, savoring his own beauty. Then she stepped closer and ran her hands down his chest. He was not actually completely hairless below the neck, she realized, probably because of his human ancestry. A very fine down of short, sparse hairs the same color as his brows and lashes dusted his chest and belly. She bent and licked a nipple, eliciting a gasp and a moan.

Glancing down, Adara gulped when she saw the size of the bulge in Lemas' codpiece. He was, after all a very big man. Not so bulky as all that, but the better part of a foot taller than Stellan. It stood to reason that, if he were built proportionately, his member would be huge.

Lemas undid the buttons and began peeling off his leggings with the attached codpiece, standard garb for males across most of Tanar. His cock, freed at last of its restraints, sprang out perpendicular to his flat, muscular belly. Gee, he even had some pubic hair! Like the rest of his hair except on the top of the head, it was dark brown and quite fine. But where Adara's was curly, the little patch of hair immediately above that jutting purple-headed monster was nearly straight.

She was using this clinical inspection of her new lover to distract herself from the insistent member glowing less than a foot away from where she stood, pointing accusingly at her belly. Gods, what a thing! It was not only close to a foot long, but proportionately thick. Feeling a little trepidation, Adara stepped close to kiss Lemas and seized his erection in her hand, squeezing firmly.

He gave another gasp, and Adara eased off a little. She was determined to have him inside her when he came, and while she had never been with a virgin before she guessed that he probably wasn't going to have much self-control. Whispered conferences with some of her peers in Pine Hill had revealed stories of boys who came in their pants while they were trying to get undressed, too eager to hold back. Supposedly that situation got better with age.

Well, she'd already had a nice orgasm. Why make the poor boy wait any longer? She took him by the hand, and led him over to the bed. "Lie down," she told him, and he did as bidden. He still seemed entranced by the sight of her naked body, gazing at her in near-awe as she came over to lie beside him.

They lay on their sides facing one another, kissing passionately as his stiff cock was pressed between them. It was so hot! "All right," Adara said after another minute. She rolled over onto her back. Other positions could wait for lesson two, she figured. She spread her legs wide apart, knees up.

"Kneel between my legs and push your cock inside me, slowly," Adara commanded. Lemas wasn't about to disobey, though the "slow" part was hard to manage. It was so tight, so hot, so wet and slippery inside there, so…! "Aaaah," Adara sighed as that enormous shaft with its cushiony, swollen head worked its way inside. When it was a little more than halfway in, she told him "Pull out a little, then back in a little more, nice and easy."

Easy?! Lemas balls were screaming at him, the sensations from his cock so intense and his excitement so great that he was no longer able to listen to instruction. He plunged deeply into Adara as she wrapped her legs around his hips, and began moving in and out until his climax crashed over him like a tidal wave. He had masturbated many times through adolescence and his lonely young adulthood, but it had never felt like this!

Sunk full-length inside Adara, feeling as if he might have filled her to the brim with his seed, he held her tightly in his arms and covered her face with kisses. Adara was shaken, swept away by Lemas' passion and her own. Oh, what had she gotten herself into?

Adara had half expected Lemas to soften and pull out, uncorking what felt like an ocean of cum onto the bedsheets, and start spouting boyish declarations of love and gratitude. What happened instead was that he remained inside her, kissing her with growing passion and skill. In about a minute he was rock-hard again, and lesson two had begun in earnest.

An hour later Adara and Lemas lay side by side on the bed with his head on the pillow while hers was pillowed on his shoulder. She felt as if she had been run over by a horsecart, after coming half a dozen times and introducing Lemas to several new positions. She was going to be sore in the morning, she knew it. Her new lover seemed to combine the energy and enthusiasm of Stellan with a cock that was half again the size. Whoof!

Now, finally, there was time for talk about more important matters. "How go your researches at the Royal Library?" Lemas asked softly. He seemed to be as exhausted, and as satisfied, as was Adara.

"I've been through everything the crown confiscated from the archives at Meruzal," she replied. "The bulk of it was from much more recent times, I'm afraid. But I did find a reference to that last battle of the war between the merudur and pinudur. And I think I know where to find Queen Myralis' tomb."

Lemas lifted his head from the pillow to turn and look at her, his features animated. "Really? Wow, that would be so amazing!" Prizal was not just a historically important artifact and a fabulous treasure. It was one of the most iconic items in the history of smithing among the merudur, the very first irilium sword crafted by the smith who had originated that art among their people. For elven smiths such as Lemas, it was hard to imagine anything more worth finding.

Adara smiled up at him, her eyes heavily lidded. The wine had long since worn off, burned away by all the exercise she'd gotten; but she felt exhausted, and ready to sleep. "All of the honored merudur dead from that battle were interred together in a sort of stone crypt," she explained. "And when it was completed they buried it in the earth, as a monument and to keep out grave robbers. A friend of mine visited a similar sort of tomb, but built by humans and much more recently, not that far from Carlienne. It seems to have been a popular technique."

"And where is it?" Lemas asked eagerly. His cock lay quiescent now, a sleeping snake sprawled across one thigh. Even in repose it was something to behold.

"On the east side of the coastal plain in Elvany where the battle was fought, overlooking the sea," she explained.

"So you're going to Elvany to search for it?"

"Now that I have Sierlas there's no reason to put off leaving," Adara replied sleepily. "I'll have to gather some supplies and make a few arrangements, but I should be ready to leave by early day after tomorrow. I'll have to go down to the docks to catch a ferry to Sandham and then travel along the coast road for a couple of days. I can come visit you at the forge on my way to the docks."

No reason to put off leaving? Lemas thought bleakly. What am I, chopped bait? He quickly banished the thought. Adara had warned him from the beginning that their liaison couldn't lead to anything long-term, and he knew it was insane to fall in love with her. He would still be a young elf centuries after she'd died of old age. But deep inside, he knew common sense didn't have anything to do with the way he felt. "I want to come with you," he said quietly.

# Chapter 9

Adara had expected Falodar to raise a host of reasons why Lemas could not come along. He'd seen his own son fall for a human woman and endure all the heartache such unions must produce: two of their three children moving away and now long dead; watching his young consort become a tottering crone, and nursing her through her life's end as if she were a beloved grandparent – less than a century after the passion of their love had begun. "You can't know how sweet it was, Father," Niemas had told him. "It was worth everything we both had to go through, and look at Lemas. Is he not reward enough for our suffering?"

And then there was the fact that Lemas was Falodar's apprentice – theoretically bound to live at the smithy and work without pay other than room and board and a little spending money. Surely he could not just drop his responsibilities and run off adventuring?

But Adara had reckoned without the lure of the Sword of Myralis. To Falodar as it was to Lemas, the chance to lay hands on that fabled artifact was worth whatever it took. And he himself could hardly run off adventuring. He knew the boy had fallen in love with the young woman, and he regretted the pain that was undoubtedly going to cause for all concerned; but from the perspective of his many centuries of life, he knew that the pain of lost love wasn't all *that* hard to get over. Even when your consorts didn't die of old age but just got tired of you and left (as three of his had, over the years), it hurt. And then you moved on.

So on the morning of the day two days after Adara and Lemas' first joining, the pair were packed and ready to go. Adara had visited the stable where she and Ferdyn had bought Zarhya and Simdal, and chatted up Daniel Hostler. After a few minutes of negotiation she'd bought a tall, sturdy young mule named Debardo. For this journey Lemas (who assured her he had ridden, often, back home in Elyrion) would ride Sadiq. A man his height might better have been mounted on a destrier, but the Khoureshi breed were no ponies. He would do.

Ferdyn had cheerfully agreed to let Adara continue to store various of her belongings, especially all the wardrobe items she had no need of, at his townhouse. She thought he secretly hoped that these things would keep her coming back – to his home, and to his arms. But she'd declined to hop into the sack with him one more time before taking her leave. She was, it seemed, a serial monogamist.

Lemas had put in one more full day of work at the smithy and gathered the things he would need for their expedition, joining Adara that evening at the King's Arms for another delicious supper – and an even more delicious lovemaking session – before bed. She had indeed been feeling a little sore in the morning, but by evening she'd been ready for more of what Lemas had to offer. He was so powerful, so passionate, and so sincere that he utterly overrode every objection she had to being with him. She sighed as she thought about it. She knew there was heartache ahead, but you only live once.

Malika, who'd preferred riding on the front of Zarhya's saddle when they were traveling since the day Adara had rescued her, curiously formed an immediate bond with Debardo. As their little party set out from the inn's stable yard on their way to the docks, she was happily perched atop the canvas and leather baggage packs the mule had been fitted with. Adara had suggested to her, silently, that it would be a good idea not to be seen flying around Carlienne in daylight. There might well be people down there in the streets armed with bows.

They stopped in to say farewell to Falodar, and he wished them success with their venture. Adara had offered Voleur to Lemas, but it turned out he had his own sword – two inches longer than the bastard sword, also of gleaming steel. She'd left the old sword, which she wasn't yet emotionally ready to part with, along with the rest of her unneeded belongings at Ferdyn's. Lemas owned no armor, but Falodar had lent him a steel breastplate to wear over his traveling leathers.

The ferry ride south across the length of Carlienne Bay to the docks at Sandham took a couple of hours, and Adara was glad that the day was not too windy. She'd only been on the open water one other time, at the end of the riverboat ride she'd taken from Grandwyl with Ferdyn, and had felt rather queasy. This time it hit her stomach a little harder, and she shuddered to think what it must be like during a storm. Lemas, smiling at the whitecaps gleaming beneath the glittering spring sun, showed no hint of such problems. The merudur were all seafarers, and he'd been out on boats in the Westwater near his childhood home for decades.

It was with great relief on Adara's part that they stepped off the ferry at Sandham docks, and went on their way through the town. She had held onto her breakfast, and that was a triumph. Now they had a long, slow journey on horseback as they picked up the coast road several blocks inland and then turned west, following it for a couple of miles until they had cleared the outskirts of Sandham and could pick up the pace.

The coast road through Cornmarch was one of the duchy's major thoroughfares, with much commerce going north and south a mile or so inland from the Westwater shore. Cliffs ran along for many miles there, with the occasional smugglers' cove but only one real harbor – the bay at Meruzal – north of the point where the Westwater met the Surden Sea. Sandham was one of Cornmarch's most important seaports, and goods from all over the duchy were traded for goods arriving on ships from elsewhere. Even after they'd left the small city behind, traffic was fairly heavy and they were constantly needing to nudge the horses into a canter to get around slow-moving freight wains.

At least all this traffic meant that there were inns aplenty along the coast road, conveniently spaced for travelers. Many little market villages and towns had sprung up as well, and their trip was easy and uneventful. The terrain was mostly level, the weather was dry, and no bandits threatened them. They put up for the night in a coaching inn in Remien, which sat at a distance of about a mile from the road beside a small stream that came down out of the distant hills.

Adara had not spent many hours on horseback at one time in more than a month, and Lemas was even rustier. He hadn't ridden at all since leaving Elyrion late last year. They both arrived at the inn feeling stiff and sore. Anticipating this, she had brought along a good collection of potions including some of Nanny Selden's patent liniment. They had fun giving each other backrubs, then moved on to front rubs and other activities before going to sleep. As she lay in Lemas' arms, drifting toward unconsciousness, Adara was glad he'd come along. She would have been lonely – and horny – without him.

They breakfasted early the next morning, and had the innkeeper pack them a picnic lunch before leaving. The day had dawned gray and blustery, with a stiff onshore breeze, but so far no rain had fallen as they started off at a good clip heading south. Before they stopped to eat their fruit and sandwiches they were traveling in the area known as Elvany, though there were no signs to mark the transition.

The area of coastline, some hundred-fifty miles from north to south and going back inland seventy-five miles to the eastern hills, was officially just a part of Cornmarch – a duchy of the kingdom of Tanar. But it was here, at Meruzal, that the ancient merudur kingdom of Silaine had had its capital in the time of Queen Myralis. Thousands of years later, after Silaine had become Elyrion, a large population of elves still remained.

Adara and Lemas were heading for Meruzal, and expected to reach it before nightfall. In the morning they'd make their way to the plain of Gadsen south and east of the city, where that legendary battle had been fought. But for now, they had hours of riding ahead of them.

As they trotted along, Adara asked "Was it the current king of Elyrion who got your people into a war over this land, Lemas?" He nodded.

"Our rulers, kings or queens, are chosen by the clan chieftains when they meet at the Royal Moot every hundred years. King Tersin of the Belesion clan was elected forty-two years ago. He was quite popular when he demanded that the merudur majority in Elvany should be granted self-rule and independence from Tanar, back when I was still an adolescent. But his popularity kind of fell off after the Tanar army kicked our butts back to Elyrion and sacked Meruzal."

He said that with a wry grin. Adara frowned. "Since you can choose your king, I'm surprised the clan chieftains didn't boot him out of office. Couldn't they do that, if the ruler turned out to be completely useless?"

"Technically, yes," Lemas replied. "But you have to remember, my people are really conservative. They don't like to rock the boat or change the way things are done – and it's been thousands of years since the current system was put into place. That's the way they did it in Queen Myralis' time, and while some people are agitating to call a special moot, most would rather just wait. It's not as if ousting Tersin would change what happened twenty-odd years ago."

"Good point," Adara admitted. It seemed like a good system, possibly better than the one in Tanar where the eldest son (or daughter, if there were no sons) of the current ruler would automatically become the next one – regardless of their qualifications for the job. King Arden had ruled for most of Adara's life and he was all right, she supposed – the kingdom prospered, and most people were happy enough with its laws. But suppose his son turned out to be a drunkard or a fool?

"So, what was so special about the Sword of Myralis, anyway?" Adara asked, moving to a new subject.

"It was the first irilium sword forged by the merudur, for one thing," Lemas replied. "That was a really big deal back then. The scattered human tribes in Eorla were armored in hide or bronze, and some of them were just starting to learn how to smelt iron. And the pinudur were behind us in the use of irilium. It was a huge advantage for us to have weapons, even if it were just one sword, that could cut through anything the enemy had."

Adara mused on this. It was a wonder humans ever managed to drive the merudur off the continent, considering this discrepancy in their military technology. But the force of numbers must have won out. "And this Prizal had enchantments on it, too?" Cruztan Milegos had told Ferdyn that his longsword Virago, claimed from the tomb of an ancient warlord when he was little older than Adara was now, had been enchanted with unbreakability – making it in some ways the equal of any irilium blade. In addition, it conveyed untiring strength in battle and a superior level of fighting skills to whoever was wielding it. Ferdyn, armed with that blade, had cut his way through a dozen or more armed and armored Swinzen in the stronghold of the Mancer King last year.

"The exact list of enchantments isn't known, really," Lemas replied as they rode along at a light canter. "Since the sword's been lost for so long, along with many of the written records from that time, it's down to legend. It was said that Prizal granted its wielder absolute dominance on the field of battle – that no foe could stand before it."

"Yet Queen Myralis was killed in that battle," Adara mused.

"Right," Lemas replied. "That would seem to put the lie to the legend. But maybe it only enabled you to defeat enemies who were facing off against you with bladed weapons. In the heat of battle, she might have been struck from behind with a poisoned dagger, or hit by arrow fire. Irilium armor hadn't been developed, yet."

"Well, maybe we'll find out tomorrow," Adara responded. "Wouldn't that be fine?" He grinned at her, and they continued on their way. They entered the ruined outskirts of Meruzal as evening was coming on. The city had been walled for millennia, but in the aftermath of the Elvany War when Meruzal was taken and sacked, King Johan had decreed that the walls be torn down and the stone taken away. There had been much rebuilding in the decades since, but even though Meruzal Bay was the only halfway decent harbor on the Westwater south of Carlienne Bay, the city was still scarcely half the size it had been a century before.

The merudur population of Elvany was half what it had been, as well. Some few of the elves, living within the kingdom of Tanar for generations, had sided with the country to which they technically belonged. But most had joined the uprising, and many who survived the conflict had emigrated to Elyrion after the war. The elven defeat had been a humiliation that was hard to swallow, and for many the hostile environment of the mainland had been unacceptable. Still, there were more merudur living in this region than anywhere else in Tanar.

So when Adara and Lemas checked in at the Evardilon, a hostelry a quarter of a mile inland from the docks, it was she and not he that got the questioning looks. The innkeeper was merudur, a woman of indeterminate age with snow-white hair worn in a long braid down her back and skin the color of skim milk. She eyed Lemas with interest and Adara with suspicion, but accepted her money readily enough.

It was late for a meal, but they were able to get hearty bowls of fish chowder and some bread that wasn't too stale. They washed it down with a chilled Elyrion white wine and sat talking quietly in the common room after eating. The architectural style of this inn was utterly different from any Adara had seen before, all built of painted timber with high, vaulted ceilings and decorative friezes running everywhere. From what she'd seen of elves so far, all of them – even the kobolds – were possessed of artistry. Perhaps it was something you naturally gravitated toward, if you had enough time.

They were hanging out here through the later part of the evening, not because of any desire for entertainment or company – even after a long day on the road, they'd rather have been upstairs having stupendous sex. Lemas had thought for decades about sex, obsessed about it in his adolescence; and now that he had finally experienced it, and with a beautiful girl who haunted his thoughts during every waking moment, he was eager to keep having it. A lot.

No, they sat there slowly sipping the dry white wine with their ears sharply tuned to the conversations around them. Somewhat to Adara's surprise, the majority of those conversations were not in Franca, as you might expect, but in Merudur. And she could understand them. While there were differences between the ancient language she'd studied and the modern tongue, her practice sessions with Falodar and Lemas over the past week appeared to have helped her to learn both. It seemed to Adara that the elven tongue had not changed nearly as much in thousands of years as the tongues of men. No doubt because of those long lives, again.

Nobody in here was plotting treason against the crown, which was just as well. Adara was not a political person, and it would have been really annoying to uncover some plot for a second Elvany rebellion and have to go report it to the authorities. But then surely, such plotters would not be having their discussions in the common room of an inn, in the hearing of a human subject of the realm who was accompanied by an elf.

What they were listening for was any mention of Queen Myralis, the fabled Prizal, the nearby battlefield, or the ancient barrow mound Adara's studies had revealed as the site of the warrior-queen's final resting place. What they heard was complaints about the weather, the falling price of salt fish, and concerns that a ship due in two days earlier had failed to arrive. After an hour of this, satisfied that no one here at least was on the same quest they were, they went upstairs to bed.

# Chapter 10

In the morning Lemas wanted to make love again, but Adara was too excited. She wanted to be on the road to Gadsen, identifying that mound, and figuring out how to get inside it as early as possible. "But look what I have for you," he said wistfully. He was lying on the bed naked, the covers down, with that magnificent cock standing at attention. Mmm, he *did* look good enough to eat.

So far, though Adara had initiated Lemas into many permutations of sex, she had not yet tried to give him a blow job. She doubted she would be able to get that monster very far into her mouth, though her cunt seemed to have no trouble taking him in. But maybe...

She had already put on her fine linen underwear, but was still trying to decide what to wear. She didn't want to arouse suspicions by riding off into this peaceful land armored for battle. "Maybe just a quickie," Adara said, and climbed up onto the bed to kneel beside Lemas. She kissed him on the lips, then ran her hand down his torso before seizing his erection in one hand and taking it (some of it, anyway) into her mouth. His eyes went wide.

"Gods, that feels amazing!" he exclaimed, stroking her hair as she went down on him. It was one of the first things Ferdyn had taught her, and it worked like a charm on Lemas. She stroked and squeezed the lower half of his cock while sucking and licking the head and upper part of the shaft, and with a groan he filled her mouth with his seed. Hey, elf cum tasted kind of sweet. Who knew? Maybe that was a contributing factor in their lower fertility, if the women were all motivated to give blow jobs...

A few minutes later they had gathered their belongings and repaired to the common room to check out. A much younger-looking male merudur was on duty this morning, and he accepted back the room key and arranged for the kitchen to pack them some food. They'd brought trail rations, but would prefer fresh food whenever possible. Adara, especially, had grown rather sick of the taste of trail bread. For breakfast, they had some light and airy merudur pastries baked around pockets of jam. They were delicious, but Adara wondered how well they would stick to their ribs.

Soon they had found the road leading east and set out along it. Malika had spent most of yesterday sleeping and most of the previous night flying around the waterfront area catching rats and the occasional roosting seagull. Seasides were not the semigryph's usual habitat, but they offered rich hunting grounds for a flying nocturnal predator. She had been back, sleeping in the hayloft, by the time they'd gotten the horses out this morning; and seemed quite content to curl up on Debardo's back and go right back to sleep once they had gotten underway.

The site of the ancient battlefield was around twenty miles from the current outskirts of Meruzal. In the nine thousand years since Myralis' defeat of the invading pinudur there, it had hosted other battles; but during the time that Tanar had existed as a political entity, it had been given over to agriculture. The coastal climate was often cool and windy, but milder than further inland. It did quite well for growing crops such as artichokes, cabbage sprouts, asparagus, and strawberries. The berries were all consumed locally, of course, but some of the sturdier crops were exported to other regions.

Not long after leaving Meruzal behind Adara and her party turned south onto a broad but unpaved farm track. The sky was leaden and there was a fresh breeze, but there was no scent of rain on the wind. On either side of the track were farm fields, some crops well along while others were just sprouting. They spotted a few workers, humans and elves both, engaged in weeding and watering. But none were close to the road and no one spoke to them or paid them any attention.

There was little sound but the clopping of the animals' hooves, the soughing of the wind, and the faint cries of gulls wheeling near the coast a few miles away. Adara thought that if she concentrated, she might also be able to hear the surf crashing against the cliffs. Meruzal Bay was the only major gap in a nearly unbroken line of crumbling cliffs that ran all the way from Sandham to Riveil on the Surden Sea.

Despite the peacefulness of the scene, Adara was buzzing with anxiety. What would they find? Compared with some of the quests she and Stellan had engaged in over the past few months the payoff from this might be astounding – to find an artifact so legendary it was still spoken about nine millennia after it had vanished. Maybe not quite as impressive as freeing an entire race from enslavement; but still a big deal. Yet their surroundings were so… prosaic. It was hard to imagine such a bucolic setting could yield anything worthwhile.

They were beginning to think about those sandwiches in their packs when, off to the east across the planted fields, a long, unnatural-looking hill came into view. It ran north to south, looking to be nearly five hundred feet long from end to end and as high as a two-story building. It stood miles from the range of hills that formed the eastern border of Elvany, and was thickly overgrown with spring grass and wildflowers.

"That has to be it!" Lemas said excitedly, and Adara nodded with a nervous smile. She was much more comfortable raiding tombs if they were out in the middle of nowhere. Suppose some passing farmer came to ask them what the hell they thought they were doing? Since she was really only doing this out of historical interest, and fully intended that the fabulous sword and any other treasures she might unearth would become part of the royal treasury in Elyrion, she hoped she had nothing to worry about.

This not being ranch country, there were no fences. They came upon a narrow dirt lane heading east, and turned off the main farm road to come at the barrow mound from the south. "Did your source say how we're supposed to get into the mound?" Lemas asked. Finding the legendary Sword of Myralis would be wonderful, but he was just glad to be traveling in company with Adara instead of slaving away at his grandfather's forge. Smithing was enjoyable and valuable work, but it was not a very adventurous pursuit for a young elf newly come to manhood.

"Apparently that last battle of the war with the pinudur was a calamity for everyone concerned," Adara replied as they drew closer to their goal. "So many people were killed on both sides that it probably took several hundred years for the merudur and pinudur populations to recover, and there would have been a generation with very few men in it. The pinudur dead were burned on pyres, but the merudur who had fallen were all interred in a specially-built tomb. They didn't expect ever to open it again once it was covered in earth, but during construction it had to have a couple of doors and some ventilation."

"And we just figure out where these doors were and dig them out?" Lemas asked, wondering how *that* was supposed to work. Adara had demonstrated some surprising powers. Did she have the ability to see into solid earth?

"I'm hoping we won't have to dig," she replied. She had never tried to get Nomen to do something like this before, and would never have tried it if she were on the *inside* of the tomb. But she figured if there was some subsidence it wouldn't matter. Nobody in there but dead people, after all.

They reached the northern end of the mound, which sloped up gradually to a broad ridge, and dismounted for a picnic amidst the grass and wildflowers. Lemas eyed Adara as he sank his teeth into the sandwich packed by the cook at the Evardilon, in his imagination laying her down in the fragrant tall grass and making love to her for hours. Perhaps if the weather were nicer...

But his lover had been all business since they'd gotten up this morning. What she had done to him with her hands and mouth had been a pleasant surprise, but he was hoping a positive outcome for today's archaeological investigations might put her in the mood for something more. Given his preference, they'd be spending all day and all night in bed together, every day.

After eating they relieved Debardo of his heavy pack, and let the animals graze on the slopes while they began exploring the mound. Malika, suddenly alert, had launched herself as soon as they arrived and begun a series of short, hopping flights above the mound searching for movement. From time to time she stooped, and had caught two or three voles by the time Adara and Lemas had finished with their own lunch.

Adara and Lemas strapped their swords to their backs before beginning to explore the mound. The grass was somewhat taller on the broad top, thinner on the sides where erosion had taken its toll. But other than the unnatural shape, there were no signs of a stone structure beneath the soil. Nine thousand years, and the soil had not eroded enough to expose what lay beneath it! It was enough to make Adara think some magic must be involved. Wasn't Myralis' consort,

Rohiran, supposed to have been a magus? This tomb might have been his last tribute to the woman he loved.

As they reached the top and began looking around, Malika came in for a landing and sent a question at Adara. What's up? Looking for holes, Adara sent back, but got the mental equivalent of a shrug for reply. Hmm... Then she had a thought. Gophers! The busy little creatures tunneled everywhere, staying safe from surface predators while seeking the plant roots they ate.

Rather than have Lemas hold her elbow, Adara folded herself down to sit cross-legged amid the grass and flowers. "I'm going to search for little creatures who might help me locate what we're looking for," she told him, and he nodded. In their many long talks over the past week she'd mentioned her riding ability.

Adara sent her awareness out, finding it helpful to close her eyes against the glaring gray light as she pinpointed the little creatures that were living on the barrow mound. There were a lot of them! Unlike the farm fields that surrounded it, this area was never disturbed by plows – an ideal location for mice and other rodents to make their burrows and raise their families.

Only the gophers dug substantial tunnels, and she slipped into one's mind as it was scrabbling away at the earth, busily connecting a new line in the labyrinth of such tunnels that crisscrossed the top surface of the mound. She mentally chided herself as she tried to look through its eyes and realized (of course) that it was utterly dark inside the tunnel. Only its senses of smell, hearing, and feel guided the little burrower as it tunneled through the earth.

Bending it to her will, Adara sent the gopher tunneling down at a sharper angle. It was curious, she realized, that no trees had sprouted here in all the millennia since the soil had been laid on and tamped down. The roots of such would surely have burrowed far deeper than the gophers would have, likely working their way into cracks and eventually causing the underlying stone of the barrow to crumble.

That guessed-at magic spell again? Or maybe it was just that the climate and soil here weren't conducive to the growth of trees. On the entire plain, the only ones in sight had been planted as windbreaks or were growing alongside the little watercourses that flowed west to the sea in a few places.

The gopher was digging as fast as it could, but was frequently required to turn around and shove the dirt back out to a side tunnel. Lemas, wondering what was going on in Adara's mind as she sat with her eyes closed, shrugged and wandered off to see what he could find for himself. He pulled out his sword from his sheath and began prodding with it whenever he spotted a bare patch in the earth, or one that seemed a little sunken.

The soil of the coastal plain was sandy, but it appeared that the ancient merudur might have brought the dirt covering the mound from further afield. It seemed to have a relatively high clay content, and below the relatively thin layer of topsoil in which the grasses and herbs were rooted it was hard as stone. At least, Lemas assumed it was hard as stone. What if he had actually struck the stone of the tomb?

Adara remained unmoving, and Lemas hiked back down the slope and took a spade from the pack that was lying on the ground near where the horses and pack mule were grazing. He carried it back to where he'd been poking with the sword, a bare and slightly sunken patch around two-thirds of the way south from where they'd climbed up, and began digging a hole.

He soon struck stone, but it was not masonry. More like rocks twice the size of his fist, which had been mixed in with clay soil when the tomb had been buried. That helped to account for the fact that thousands of years of rain had not eroded the mound down to the structure of the tomb, he supposed, sighing. What now?

Just then Adara opened her eyes and got to her feet. "It seems as if the tomb is about ten feet below the surface here on top," she reported. "I think it's time for us to go back down and try Plan B."

"The dirt beneath the top layer is hardpan full of big rocks," Lemas informed her. "I guess my remote ancestors really didn't want this place broken into."

She smiled wryly at him, and started back down the northern slope. Malika trotted beside her for a few paces, then took to the air and soared down to land near where Debardo was grazing. She touched noses with her long-eared friend, then flopped down in a patch of short grass and began giving herself a bath.

"You're going to feel some earth tremors," Adara warned Lemas after they were back on the flat ground north of the mound, "but don't be alarmed." She reached out to the minds of the animals and sent calming thoughts, then decided it might be better to keep the horses and mule physically in check. "Let's hold their reins so they don't bolt," she suggested, and Lemas took the reins of Zarhya and Sadiq while she gathered Debardo's lead line in both hands. Then she reached out to Nomen, the earth elemental.

Since of the four this one's favors were most likely to cause risk to herself and others she didn't intend to hurt, he was the one she had contacted least in her life. But her recent experiences living underground had attuned her to his element, and he came readily to her call. A low vibration began, then became a grumbling roar as the soil of the mound seemed to twitch like the hide of a fly-bitten horse. Grass and herbs waved wildly, and little landslides started all over the surface of the mound.

Ahead of them, on the gradual north slope, a cascade of soil and rocks came rattling down and an area near the bottom fell in. Moments later the rumbling ceased, and Adara got the equivalent of a pleased "There, how's that?" from the earth elemental. The entire event had lasted for only a few seconds, but the horses were alarmed. Malika had immediately taken to the air, flying around in anxious circles.

Once again Adara sent calm, and the animals quickly settled down and returned to what they'd been doing. Lemas was staring in amazement. A great deal of the soil had come down from the east and west sides of the mound, revealing the squared-off shape of the tomb roof in places. The building was really only one tall story in height, though it might have an underground level as well. He released the reins of the now-calm horses and picked up the spade again, making for the spot of the cave-in.

# Chapter 11

Adara was rummaging through the packs getting out some more excavation tools and the Siiri glow-lamps she'd brought with her, when she heard a sharp cry from Lemas and whirled to see what was wrong. He was wielding his spade like a weapon, holding it threateningly over his head, and staring down into the hole with eyes wide.

"There's… something… down there!" he cried. "I was digging and something tried to grab the spade out of my hand!" Uh oh. Adara recalled Ferdyn's tale of his first time as a tomb raider, and how he'd been warned by the locals that the barrow mound he was breaking into was haunted by undead guardians. He'd found none, nor anything all living in the buried tomb where air was a scarce commodity. But that didn't mean all such tombs were free of sorcerous protection.

Joining Lemas at the hole and setting down her digging tools, Adara drew Sierlas and peered down. It appeared there had been a door on this end of the tomb, one with a portico made of stone slabs. One of those slabs had fallen in, and the resultant hollow was half-full of dirt rubble from the hillside – sifting down into a dark space to the south.

Keeping her eyes open and a tight grip on her sword, Adara sent her awareness out and down, into the opened tomb. There were a number of sentient creatures inside, but their glow was not the same as that of a normal living being. Was it because they were actually undead? Air seemed to be moving from behind her into the darkness below, and she guessed that this was not the only breach in the tomb's outer shell. That was good, because it meant they'd be able to search the place thoroughly without worrying about running out of air to breathe. But that might just be the *least* of their worries.

"Did the merudur practice necromancy, Lemas?" Adara asked. He nodded grimly.

"It's always been kind of frowned on, but my people – or the udur in general at least – are the ones who discovered how to use magic first. There are practitioners of every kind of magic there is in Elyrion, and Rohiran was a famous magus. Supposedly since he was

64

also a smith, he focused on the arts of enchanting weapons and armor. But he might have had other skills."

"So he could have bespelled the dead merudur warriors to rise again and defend the tomb of their queen?" Adara asked, with a sinking feeling. If those warriors had been set walking in death, likely the only way you could stop them from attacking you would be to hack them limb from limb. Maybe this wasn't going to work, after all?

"I've read that such spells exist," Lemas admitted. "The legend of the Sword of Myralis doesn't mention it, and nobody has used any spell like that in thousands of years that I've heard of, but I suppose it's possible." He shuddered. Senses on the alert, they heard a faint scrabbling coming from the darkness beyond the cave-in. Then suddenly a mailed hand and arm appeared, and a figure began trying to climb up the rubble-strewn slope.

Adara and Lemas backed off, aghast, and watched as the creature struggled to free itself from the hole. It was covered from head to foot in armor made from steel and leather, a mixture of chain and plate. Only the face was visible, and it was thin and wasted but not skeletal or mummified. Whatever spell allowed this apparently dead thing to move with purpose had preserved both its flesh and its armor, which should have been nothing but a heap of rust and powdered fragments of dried leather after nine thousand years underground.

As it finally made its way far enough up the shifting pile of dirt and climbed out of the hole, Lemas spoke to it in Merudur. The modern tongue was similar enough that perhaps it could understand. "Stop! Who are you?" Surprisingly the figure did stop. It looked around it in confusion. Then it focused on Lemas, lifted its sword, and came on in a stumbling gait.

"Wait! I am merudur as are you, a descendant of your people!" Lemas tried next. It was at least half-true, after all. Again the undead warrior hesitated. It drew in a breath. And then, in a voice like the rustling of dead leaves, it spoke. "I... I am Talion of clan Nibarian. I must... serve and defend. One of the chosen... Our Lady's Guardians... failed, but not again. You shall not pass."

Talion came on again sword swinging. As Lemas raised his own weapon to block, Adara brought Sierlas around from the side. The glistening irilium blade sliced through the chainmail hanging from the back of his helmet, and through flesh and bone to remove the Guardian's head from his shoulders. He fell forward on the turf, and did not stir again.

Surprisingly, there had been a brief gout of blood. Eyes wide, Adara re-sheathed the sword and approached the fallen warrior for a closer inspection. As she did so, Lemas gasped. Before their eyes the figure was melting away, steel armor becoming rust, flesh becoming bone, bones becoming dust. Before she could move two steps, there was nothing lying on the ground but a heap of unrecognizable detritus. Clearly, whatever spell had preserved the ancient warrior and his accouterments had been removed with his head.

Adara crouched and took a pinch of the stuff in her hand, rubbing it between thumb and forefinger as the powder wafted away on the onshore breeze. She rose to her feet and dusted off her hands. Then she smiled. "That wasn't as hard as I thought it was going to be," she admitted wryly.

"You read about these 'Our Lady's Guardians'?" Lemas asked, and she nodded.

"They were the queen's personal bodyguard," she replied. "Pretty much every monarch I've ever read about who took the field of battle had a group of elite soldiers around them, tasked with keeping their leader alive. I guess things must have gone badly for Talion and his fellow chosen when the queen died on their watch."

Lemas stared from the pile of dust and rust to the hole, and then looked at Adara. "So you think that all of the Guardians got put on eternal watch here after death?" he asked thoughtfully.

"That's my guess," she replied. "I'm not sure exactly how many of them there were, but surely not that many. And if all we have to do is behead them, they shouldn't be that hard to defeat. Are you ready to give it a try?"

One of the things he loved about her was her cheerful confidence. And here he was, a big strong man. How could he say no? They took the time to put on what armor they had before climbing down into the hole, though. Adara thought maybe Malika might be willing to do a little reconnaissance for them, but the semigryph took one sniff at the entrance to the tomb and sent a strong "No way!"

They spent a few minutes with their spades at the collapsed northern entrance of the tomb, ridding it of loose soil and rocks and tamping down what remained into a ramp that allowed an easy path up and down. During this time, no further Guardians showed up.

"Maybe old Talion had the door sentry position," Adara mused as they each took a Siiri hand-lamp and stepped down onto the stone floor of the tomb. It appeared to be built from dressed blocks of the same stone the cliffs were made of – not nearly as hard or sturdy as granite, but hard enough it seemed. There was a lot of dampness in the air, and a pervasive chill. Here and there they could hear water dripping.

The layout of the tomb building was simple – a long corridor ran straight down the middle from the door they'd come in at to a similar, still-buried entrance on the south end. Every fifty feet, open doorways stood on either side of the corridor leading to rooms in which the corpses of the honored merudur dead rested in stone alcoves stacked three high.

The Siiri hand lamps were not actually made by the Siiri, but used Siiri technology. Adara and Stellan had found a stash of the orange-glowing disks that were used to provide light by being embedded in walls throughout Zabran Lokaini, and mounted them on hollow boxes with a disk on each of the four sides and a handle for carrying. Unlike the ones within the subterranean city, these glowed with a dim light all the time – instead of brightening during the day and shutting down at night. The adventurers had found them very useful on some of their excursions since, but when Stellan left her he hadn't taken his.

They had reached the halfway point of the corridor, and in each of the mausoleums they had found only piles of rust and dust. With the dampness down here, the honored dead and all their possessions had dissolved away to nothing over the millennia. At the center point of the building, short corridors led to stairways going down – the place *did* have a lower level!

As they debated which way to go, they heard shuffling steps approaching from the far end of the central corridor – another Guardian? They set their lamps down on the stone floor, and drew their swords as the warm light glimmered off the approaching warrior's polished steel armor. They didn't try to speak with this one, nor did he (or might it have been she?) strike up a conversation.

The corridor was only ten feet wide, tight quarters for two to fight side by side. Adara called Salomand, and as a gout of flame sprang up in the ancient Guardian's face, she used the distraction to slip around behind him. There was nothing flammable to burn, and in seconds the fire had gone out. The warrior had spotted Adara's movement out of the corner of his eye, but as he turned toward her Lemas came at him from the side with a slashing longsword attack.

The undead warrior parried, but the chainmail of his hauberk and the leather beneath it was scored. Only Adara's sword was hard and sharp enough to cut through steel armor as if it were hard cheese, and as soon as the Guardian was focused on Lemas she bore down hard on a diagonal cut that split their foe from the right shoulder where it joined the neck to halfway down the torso.

Again, there was a brief fountain of blood. Sierlas' blade was stuck tight, but came free readily enough a few moments later when this warrior dissolved into dust as Talion had. Adara pulled a handkerchief from a pocket and used it to wipe the blade before re-sheathing it. There had been liquid blood there for a few seconds, but it had turned to dust like the rest of the corpse.

"Nice teamwork," Lemas said with a grin. He'd trained with weapons of all kinds through his adolescence because that was what boys in Elyrion, especially the grandsons of smiths, were supposed to do. You couldn't make weapons for others without knowing how to use them yourself. But today was the first time he'd ever faced a living foe. Well, sort-of living…

They picked up their lamps again and continued down the central corridor to the south. In a couple of spots along the corridor, and in two of the mausoleum rooms, they spotted dots of wan light on the floor that turned out to be daylight issuing through holes in the ceiling. But they found no further Guardians.

"Only two of them on this floor," Adara said thoughtfully. "Shit, that probably means all the rest of them are clustered around Queen Myralis downstairs."

"Too bad you couldn't talk Malika into coming down for a look-see," Lemas remarked.

Hey wait, there was an idea. Standing near the stairs leading down to the east, Adara quested out once again. The local wildlife (save a few gophers who'd been buried alive in their tunnels and suffocated) had recovered by now from the terror generated by the earth tremors earlier. In an area with so many small rodents, there ought to be something that eats them... There!

Curled up in his den, the stoat suddenly found himself awake and in a dreamlike state. He didn't know why, but he felt compelled to come out in the daylight and make his way hurriedly to the new hole that had appeared in the earth near the mound where he usually caught his supper of an evening. He slipped inside, and in less than five minutes had joined Adara and Lemas where they stood waiting at the head of the stairs.

Adara pulled a little hunk of trail bread out of her pack and fed it to the oversized weasel, anxious that he shouldn't run out of steam before completing his mission. It was bizarre, being simultaneously in her own head and body and in that of the stoat. When she felt the surge of energy the high-protein, high-fat treat had provided begin to course through the furry little body, she sent her emissary slinking down the stairs for a look around.

Damn, it was too dark! She'd hoped that tapping the resources of a mostly nocturnal creature might enable her to see more; but not even a bat can see in total darkness. She brought it back up, and dug a different sort of lamp out of her pack. This had been given to her by Ghryzindion of the Karindi, the once and future kobold trader, and it was just a metal rod with a cluster of blue-glowing phorium crystals on the end of it.

The stoat, its motivations entirely at her command, picked up the rod in its mouth and returned down the stairs once again. It did a quick circuit of the lower level, as Adara sat down on the stone floor and closed her eyes. The light of the phorium rod was so dim, the much brighter light from their orange-glowing lamps was too distracting.

Lemas watched her worriedly, not sure what was going on but willing to wait patiently at her side while it happened. The lower level of the tomb, it seemed, was also built of that same hard sandstone. As above, a long central corridor led north and south with mausoleum rooms giving off of it on either side. Nothing was stirring.

But unlike the upstairs area, the lower level had another corridor leading away from the center point, where the northern staircase came down. It ran off at right angles due east, vanishing into darkness. The stoat hurried along it, beginning to pant at the unaccustomed exertion. Mustelids had manic energy and ferocity aplenty, but not all that much stamina.

Abruptly the corridor opened out into a broad chamber, too large to be completely lit by the dim glow of the phorium torch. Adara was just able to see that there were catafalques running along the sides of the room, with stone coffins sitting on them. And near the front entrance, between it and a larger central catafalque that Adara was willing to believe would hold the remains of Queen Myralis, were three stone chairs with tall merudur warriors seated in them. As Adara's stoat drew closer for a better look, the eyes of the one in the middle suddenly snapped open. He rose to his feet, glaring at the small intruder, and his blade came down with a crunch.

"Ouch!" Adara exclaimed involuntarily, eyes popping open. Lemas was at her side in an instant.

"Are you well?" he asked solicitously. She shook herself, and rose to her feet.

"Fine," she said. "But I hate when that happens. Good news, there are apparently only three more of those Guardians downstairs. But they're huddled around the queen's tomb, and one of them killed my scout." Lemas patted her shoulder sympathetically.

"Let's go take revenge, shall we?" he suggested.

They picked up their lamps, keeping their swords to hand, and crept down the stairs. Sierlas was the same general size and shape as Voleur but quite a bit lighter. In a pinch Adara could wield her one-handed. There was no need for them to explore the rest of the lower level, and they headed straight down the corridor that led to the queen's burial chamber.

They hadn't gotten there yet when they beheld two of the Guardians coming toward them in the orange glow, and quickly set the lamps down on the floor near the walls where they could cast some light without getting tripped over. These two both appeared to be men, as tall at least as was Lemas and wielding longswords that gave them some advantage in reach over Adara. But their armor was no better than that of their fallen fellows, and the swords were just steel.

As Lemas engaged the man on the right, Adara took on his companion. This corridor was a little wider than the one upstairs, maybe fifteen feet, and there was some room to maneuver. The Guardians must once have been the elite, the finest warriors the merudur nation could field. Yet they had not been able to prevent the death of their queen, and they had presumably been waiting here, in a state between life and death, for all the thousands of years since the tomb had been sealed. They were stiff, and slow.

Lemas brought his blade around to parry a clumsy cut, then riposted with a slash that scored the mail hauberk without piercing it. Adara was handicapped by her shorter reach, but could take advantage of her smaller stature to slip under her opponent's guard. Sierlas' blade flashed in like a darting flame, glimmering in the lamplight, and cut through the mail on his left shoulder. Blood ran red, but the warrior did not fall.

These ancient beings had red blood flowing through their veins, Adara realized. How was that possible, after thousands of years? If they'd been killed and then brought back into some unlife by a spell of necromancy, shouldn't the blood have long since ceased flowing?

These thoughts flashed through Adara's mind in an instant, even as she danced back and forth in the narrow, dimly lit space. With her irilium plate she was nearly invulnerable, though hers did not cover as much of her body as the Guardians' steel did theirs. Therefore she was doing her best to avoid getting touched by her opponent's blade.

The ancient warrior seemed to be getting warmed up, his movements becoming more fluid. Time to end this before he remembered how to fight. Adara took a step back, seeming to give him an opening. As he thrust forward, she came in beneath it and drove his blade up hard, using all her strength. He bore down harder, and with a clang the last two feet of his sword was sliced off and fell to the floor. The Guardian stared in horror at his ruined blade, then fell to the floor with a gurgle as Adara opened his throat with the tip of Sierlas.

Meanwhile Lemas was having a harder time with his own opponent. He'd taken a cut above the knee, and being armed with a blade no better than the Guardian's own he was hard pressed to make any headway against a man who had probably been practicing his swordcraft for centuries to make it into the queen's personal guard. But as his companion fell, choking on his own blood, the Guardian's attention was distracted for a fraction of a second. Lemas thrust hard, piercing the chainmail hauberk and the leather beneath it, and struck him through the heart.

He fell dead almost immediately, going to dust in less than a minute, while the man Adara had downed was still gurgling on the stone floor. She knelt and pulled his helmet from his head, releasing a fall of long, silky white hair. She felt his forehead. It was warm, or at any rate far warmer than the ambient temperature here in the lower level of the tomb. The man was alive!

Less than a minute later he choked his last and went to dust like his companion. Adara and Lemas stood side by side in the corridor, breathing hard and glancing from the mounds of dust on the floor to each other. "I don't think these warriors were ever dead," she said softly in Franca. He nodded, then shrugged.

"They are now…"

One more awaited them. They picked up their lamps, maintaining a good distance between them so that their remaining enemy could not come at both of them at once. When they reached the burial chamber they set their lamps down on the floor again, illuminating the room from front to rear.

It was bigger than any of the mausoleum rooms had been, wider and longer. On either side of the room stone catafalques bearing simply carved stone sarcophagi marched in double rows. At the very rear, on a platform laid crosswise against the far wall, was a metal casket that glimmered as if it were made of gold. Probably plated, but that plating had kept it from rotting away over the millennia.

Between them and the three stone chairs Adara had seen on her scouting expedition stood the last Guardian, his longsword held tightly in both hands. His enormous indigo eyes glittered in the lamplight. His voice squeaked like a rusty hinge, then smoothed out. Probably he had not used it in a couple of eons.

"You shall not pass," he said in ancient Merudur.

"Your companions are dead," Adara told him in the same tongue. "We are not the enemies of your people, and we are not here to rob your lady's tomb. We only seek Prizal." To their astonishment the apparition barked a short, bitter laugh.

"You seek in the wrong place," he said. "It is not here. You have only come to die."

"We killed all the rest, and we will kill you," Lemas threatened boldly. "Only let us look on Queen Myralis and we will leave you alive." Again the harsh laugh.

"Alive! Such a rare thing, to be alive. My companions and I have been alive… how long now? For we let our lady die while we yet lived, and Rohiran did decree that we would live for all eternity until we fell defending her at last. You cannot threaten me with death, stripling, for it is the thing I desire most. Come and take me if you can!"

Lemas and Adara exchanged a glance, then rushed the last Guardian from opposite sides. He barely had a chance to get his blade into play before Sierlas had taken off his head. Judgment, indeed. And a kinder one than Rohiran had meted out. Adara felt a profound horror and sadness. Had they only come here, not to die, but to set free these once-brave warriors who'd been sentenced to an eternity of unending torment?

# Chapter 12

Both of them were anxious to see what lay inside the golden sarcophagus at the back of the room, but Lemas took the time first to open one of the stone coffins. Inside was a pile of dust and rust like the five he and Adara had created since arriving here this afternoon.

"The catafalques must be the honored resting places of the Guardians who died defending their queen," Adara opined.

"And those who lived were locked away in the tomb with her for all eternity as punishment," Lemas finished for her. "Rohiran's spell must not have been necromancy but one of preservation. Something that kept the Guardians' weapons and armor intact, along with their bodies and even their minds, during all the thousands of years down here in the dark. How could they not have gone mad?"

Adara shook her head. It was beyond comprehension. "Well, I guess we'd better find out if he was lying," she said, gesturing toward the rear. They carried their lamps with them, walking slowly until they stood before the catafalque. The platform was at around hip height on Adara, the top of the sarcophagus a little above shoulder height.

She and Lemas each took an end, and nearly fell over when they discovered that the sarcophagus was neither gold, nor some baser metal, but irilium plate little thicker than normal plate armor. It weighed nowhere near as much as they had expected.

They carefully lifted the lid off and leaned it up against the wall beside the queen's catafalque. Inside the coffin, which was lined with rich blue velvet in an astonishing state of preservation, lay the body of a beautiful merudur woman. Her skin was pale blue even in the warm lamplight, and it was clear that she was truly dead. She was clad in steel plate that had been incised with filigree patterns and figured in gold and blue enamel, the most astonishingly ornate armor Adara had ever seen.

"Rohiran must have used that preservation spell on the corpse and coffin of his consort, too," Adara mused. This woman, guarded for nine thousand years by warriors who were horribly alive, was beautifully dead. Beside her in the coffin, which was at least a foot wider than her body, was a sword. It gleamed in the lamplight as

Lemas pulled it forth – polished steel, with a hilt encrusted in blue gems. The blade was smooth and unmarked – *not* an enchanted sword.

Adara stood there gazing down at the lovely corpse in sadness and frustration. Maybe they should never have come here. Now the tomb of the ancient merudur dead had been cracked open like an egg. How long before looters showed up, to steal away the fabulously valuable sword, armor, and sarcophagus? There was enough gold and irilium in that coffin to keep a family in food for a couple of years, at least.

She reached into the coffin and plucked up Myralis' hand. She was not wearing the gauntlets that had undoubtedly been part of this suit of armor when she'd worn it on the field of battle. Or had she even ever worn this on the field of battle? The armor looked intact, no sign of having been penetrated by a sword or other weapon. Maybe it had been made for her as a burial suit after her death?

There was a gold ring on the middle finger of the queen's right hand, with a carved blue stone set into it. Not much of a souvenir, but the armored body and the coffin were far too bulky and heavy for them to carry out and transport to the king's palace in Elyrion. "That's probably her signet ring," Lemas guessed.

"Might as well bring the sword too," Adara said sadly.

"What now?" he asked her, as they made their way back up the stairs and down the corridor to the door leading out.

"I have an idea," Adara replied. "I think I'll ask Nomen to work this place over a little more, collapse the entrance. We can take the ring and sword to the king in Elyrion, so the merudur people will have something to put in their treasury to remind them of their legendary queen. And if he wants me to, I can pay for a dig team to excavate the coffin and ship it home. I'm assuming that the preservation spell was intended never to expire. She might be quite an inspiring sight, lying in state in a museum where her descendants can come to see her."

Lemas pondered this. There was nothing in merudur culture to prohibit such a thing. Unlike many peoples, they had no taboos regarding the dead. "I guess that's a good idea," he said. Anything that would let him continue to travel in Adara's company was a good idea, and if she wanted to go to Elyrion she was going to need him to come along.

They stood holding the horses and mule again as the earth shook and rumbled, and the entire barrow mound sank another six feet below the height it had stood at when they'd arrived a few hours before. After the dust had dissipated, they checked to make sure there were no obvious openings. Then Adara changed back out of her armor, and applied some first aid to the sword cut above Lemas knee after he'd removed his breastplate. That done, they put the packs back on Debardo and began moving toward the narrow lane they'd come in on. Malika was soon once again sleeping atop the mule.

"That last guy we killed," Lemas said thoughtfully as they rode along. "He thought we were stupid for not knowing Prizal wasn't there in the tomb with the queen. It sounded like he knew where it actually was."

"He might have known where it went when they sealed him and his companions into that crypt," Adara pointed out, "but his information would be just a little out of date now. It could have gone anywhere in the past nine thousand years."

"The book you read didn't specifically say the sword was entombed with the queen?" Lemas asked.

"No, it didn't mention the sword at all," Adara admitted. "It just talked about the queen and the rest of the honored dead from that great battle being entombed in a barrow mound beside the battlefield, and that they burned the pinudur dead. It was my assumption from what your grandfather said that we'd find the sword interred with its owner."

"I was just thinking," he went on, "since we're going to Elyrion anyhow… There are a lot more books about merudur history there than you're ever going to find in Tanar. My stepmother knows a man who works as an archivist at the Royal Historical Archive in Prizlion. He's a friend of the family. I'm not sure, but I think maybe he used to be her consort at some point before I was born. He might be able to point us to what records we should look at. Wouldn't it be even better if we could bring Prizal to King Tersin as well as the ring and this gaudy keepsake?"

He gestured at the gleaming jeweled sword, hanging from his pack. It was clear that, in his professional opinion, it wasn't much of a sword; though it was certainly a thing of beauty. Adara shook herself out of her funk, and grinned at him. She nudged Zarhya a little closer to Sadiq and held out her left arm. "Go ahead, twist my arm," she mock-pleaded. He grinned back.

# Chapter 13

They decided to stay at a different inn for the night, thus hopefully avoiding any questions about why they'd checked out of the last one only to return hours later, covered in dust and dirt and seeking ocean passage to Elyrion. The Blue Grotto, another merudur inn somewhat closer to the waterfront (but still a respectable establishment), offered sex-separated baths similar to what Adara had enjoyed in the little hot springs town of Baadzen on her way to beard the Mancer King in his den last year.

"The Blue Grotto is actually a place in Elyrion," Lemas explained to Adara as they were walking toward the bathhouses clad in robes provided by the management. "It's a big natural cave up near the center of the island, with an underground lake in it. One of the few places outside of the Ratskells where there's much phorium. People come there from all over the island to see it."

The two of them met back at their room, pink and scrubbed and feeling a whole lot better, a little under an hour later. "I like this place better than the last one," Adara admitted. "Probably just because I really needed a hot bath. But even so…" She dropped her robe onto the bed and he dropped his on the floor, then held out his arms. She came into them with a smile.

A little over an hour after that, they were dressed and in the common room looking for supper. Earlier Adara's appetite had been adversely affected by the activities of the afternoon, but between the bath and the recent exercise she was ravenous. No surprise, the inn offered a choice of fish, prawns, or chowder. They went with the cod, which was really pretty delicious.

"How long will it take for us to get a ship for Elyrion?" Adara asked between mouthfuls. Despite what Lemas had said about the bad attitude of some of the more conservative merudur, she was excited about visiting the fabled isle of the elves. From what little elven architecture she'd seen so far, she was imagining a fairyland of beautiful landscapes and soaring, graceful structures.

"Meruzal is probably the best place anywhere near to embark from," Lemas told her. "There used to be a lot of maritime commerce between Elyrion and the ports around Carlienne Bay before the war, but now most merudur ships stay away from there. But I still don't have any idea how long it will be. We'll go down to the docks tomorrow morning early and find out what's available. Bringing along Malika and the rest of the animals is going to be harder than if we just needed passage for two people."

Adara considered. She wanted Malika with her in any case, but did they need to bring the horses? She could open a portal to Carlienne, and arrange to board the horses and mule at the stable where she'd purchased them. The whole procedure would take only a few hours. She decided to postpone that decision until after their trip to the docks in the morning.

Another thought occurred to her. "How long does it take to sail to Elyrion, anyhow?" she asked.

"From here to Prizlion, which is the major eastern port and also not that far from my father's villa, should take a couple of days and nights, depending on the weather. This time of year you can get squalls on the Westwater. But definitely less than a week."

Two days to a week, on a body of water where "you can get squalls." Erg. Was Adara signing up for days of misery? Lemas noticed her expression. "Worried about seasickness?" he asked. Her discomfort on the trip across Carlienne Bay had not gone unnoticed. Adara grimaced and nodded.

"I grew up near a little village alongside a very small river," she said. "I never experienced boat travel on the open water until around a year ago. I suppose all you merudur are naturally immune to seasickness?" Just another superiority of the elves…

He smiled at her, that boyish grin that seemed so absurdly out of place on his ethereally beautiful features – and struck her to the heart. "Not at all," he said. "Being affected by motion sickness happens to us just as much as anyone. If you spend a lot of time on the water you get used to it and it doesn't bother you anymore, that's all. But we have an excellent potion for that. I'm surprised you don't know about it, since you're an herbalist."

Adara stared at him blankly. A potion for seasickness? But then almost all she knew about herbal lore she had learned from Nanny Selden, who had lived in that same little backwater village *her* whole life. Why learn to make a potion nobody needed or wanted? "Can we buy some here?" she asked hopefully.

"I'm sure we can," he replied. "You might even be able to get the herbalist to tell you how it's made. I know it has ginger in it, but I'm pretty sure there are other ingredients as well."

They slept like logs after another lovemaking session, and were down at the docks a few blocks from the Blue Grotto by a couple of hours after sunrise. All of the sadness and disappointment of their expedition yesterday seemed to have evaporated, and Adara started the day with a positive outlook.

This outlook was somewhat dampened (literally) when they emerged from their inn to find the skies iron gray, with a light drizzle falling. Adara had heard that there were places along the Surden Sea coast of Tanar where the sun shone from blue skies on sapphire waters set against white sand beaches. That sounded like the kind of sea she'd prefer to visit. Shivering inside her cloak, she strode beside Lemas as he led the way down to the waterfront and surveyed the scene.

The Westwater coastal cliffs were broken at Meruzal by a semicircular bay; and over the millennia of inhabitation by the merudur, the harbor facilities had been improved greatly. A long stone breakwater had been added on the south entrance, to improve the shelter the bay gave from storms. The shoreline was paved in stone, and piers of stone or rockwood jutted out some two hundred feet into the bay.

Most of the vessels moored here were part of the Meruzal fishing fleet, around half of the small boats owned by humans and the rest by elves. The merudur claimed it was they who had taught the humans of Eorla modern shipbuilding, and it was probably true. There were a few larger vessels among them, three-and-four-masted trading ships. As well, the navy of Tanar kept a few warships patrolling the coast and these would sometimes be found in port.

Lemas spotted a likely-looking vessel tied up near the end of a long stone pier, and led Adara toward it. It was one of the biggest currently in the harbor, and even in this wet weather it was aswarm with sailors and dock workers, loading barrels and crates onto its decks to be taken below.

From the blue-dyed sails Adara guessed it was a merudur vessel out of Elyrion. The human mariners of Tanar believed that the natural off-white color of hempen canvas was perfectly appropriate for sails, and regarded the elves' aesthetic sensibilities as so much silliness.

A merudur man in a rain slicker stood beside a broad ramp, watching and taking notes as the workers carried their burdens up onto the ship. Lemas approached him. "What can I do for you?" he asked in Franca. The language was spoken as a trade tongue throughout Eorla, and along the northern coast of Frigan as well.

"My friend and I are seeking passage to Prizlion for ourselves. We have two horses, a mule, and a tame semigryph with us," Lemas told them. He overtopped the man by a couple of inches.

"A semigryph? What's that?" the sailor asked. They were native to the forests and rocky places of north-central Eorla, and so shy that even many people who lived within their range had never seen one. Malika was *not* a typical member of her species.

"Uh, it's sort of a small wildcat with wings," Lemas tried to explain. He'd never heard of them either, prior to meeting Adara. The sailor eyed him askance.

"I dunno about that," he said finally. "We're sailing with the tide tomorrow morning, but we don't have room for horses in any case. The captain doesn't like them crapping all over the hold. Sorry."

Adara looked a question as Lemas returned to her, and he shrugged his shoulders and shook his head. That had been the largest vessel in port at the moment, the one he'd thought likeliest. They tried the rest of the trading ships moored along the waterfront, but met with no more success. After hours of frustrated effort, they returned to their inn for lunch. Both of them were damp and out of sorts.

"There's nothing for it, then," Adara said as they sat drying beside the fire and waiting for their food to arrive. Lemas gazed at her, waiting to hear more and hoping it didn't involve giving up on their quest. This trip was the most enjoyment he'd had in his life so far, even with its occasional setbacks.

"Do you recall I mentioned Fatiha Baba to you a few days ago?" Adara asked. Lemas nodded.

"That was how you came to Carlienne from Willoughby?"

"That's right. Now that I can form a mental picture of Meruzal, I can have Fatiha Baba open a portal between here and Carlienne. I'll probably have to open it out in the country to avoid notice, so there'll be some travel time. But we can drop the horses and Debardo off for boarding at the stable where I got them. I suppose if I have to, I could get my friend Ferdyn to care for Malika while we're gone. Those two seemed to hit it off quite well. I hate to leave her, though."

"You can't just get Fatiha Baba to open a portal to Elyrion?" Lemas asked. Adara hadn't given him many details about how the djinn imprisoned within the necklace actually performed its magic. She shook her head. Just then, the barmaid arrived with a steaming platter of fish and chips, and they fell to eating – picking the hot, greasy, and delicious morsels up with their fingers and dipping them in a sweet and sour sauce.

As she chewed, Adara mused on their problem. They were going to have a busy afternoon. Then a thought occurred to her. Elves were supposed to have an affinity for magic. Did that mean that their minds possessed the strength necessary to enable the djinn to make a really large portal?

Adara licked her fingers, then wiped them on her napkin. "Lemas, can you form a mental picture of some secluded area near your childhood home?" she asked. He nodded, surprised.

"Of course I can," he said. "I lived around there for hundreds of years." She smiled slightly.

"Finish your food, then let's go to our room for a few minutes. I want to try something."

# Chapter 14

Malika was the first through the portal, scampering onto the beach with her nose twitching as she inhaled the scents of flowers and surf. Nobody around, she sent, and took to the air. "It's safe," Adara told Lemas and they put heels to their mounts and guided them through. Fatiha Baba had told Lemas that he could easily open a portal for him of whatever size he might require – the elf's mana was strong, and he had encountered no problems at all communicating mind to mind with the djinn once he wore the necklace.

They'd gone back out into the countryside away from Meruzal before opening the portal they'd traveled through, after confirming in their room that Lemas would be able to make the magic necklace work for him. Adara suspected that the powers of Fatiha Baba would be nearly as sought after as those of the Darkshield, but the former lacked the safeguards against theft that the latter had. It could be stolen by anyone, even a common cutpurse, and likely would be if very many people learned of its existence.

Yet she had trusted Lemas completely with its secret, had even handed the necklace over to him to wear. He was her lover, and her friend, and a person with a pure spirit. Once they were all standing on the soil of Elyrion – on a sandy beach in a little cove below the promontory on which stood the villa belonging to Niemas Azarion, Lemas' father – he immediately gave the djinn a mental command to close the portal. Then he took the necklace off and handed it back to her.

He was grinning. "That was a very remarkable experience," he said. "It's a good thing there aren't many of these around, or the coaching services and passenger ships would all be put out of business." Adara tucked the necklace into a pocket of her pack, and smiled back. The weather here, a couple of hundred miles away from Meruzal, was pretty much the same – gray, windy, and slightly damp.

"If the secret were to be revealed," she mused, "I imagine Fatiha Baba could open dozens of such portals all by himself – and leave them permanently open. The one to the Swinzen world had apparently been standing open for years."

"So it's only the opening of the portal that takes energy?" Lemas asked.

"I haven't actually asked," Adara admitted. "But that's what it seems like."

Lemas on Sadiq, with Debardo in tow, led the way to the southern end of the beach where a narrow trail climbed up, in a series of switchbacks, to the top of the bluff. There was a lot of vegetation up there, and the house was not visible from the beach – and vice versa.

Malika came flying in with a foot-long ocean fish of some kind wriggling in her jaws, landing on the packed sand below the tide line to devour it. She looked quite pleased with herself. Lemas grinned at the semigryph. "I think she's going to like it here," he said. Adara knew that Lemas had encountered problems with social prejudice in his homeland, but she also sensed that he was happy to be here. She supposed that no matter where your home was, or what its drawbacks, it was still home.

"I can't believe how much I've missed this place!" Lemas said cheerfully, as he led the way up the steep trail – confirming Adara's observation. Malika had finished her fresh meal and flew up to join them, landing with a gentle thump atop Debardo's packs. The stoic animal didn't flinch.

They reached the top of the trail and Adara looked in wonder on the house that Lemas had been born and grown to adulthood in. It was not particularly large, but it was beautiful! She supposed that the sort of sprawling homes the wealthy in Tanar owned would be ridiculous for people who rarely ever had more than one child. And from what Lemas had told her, the big economic divide between rich and poor that existed in Tanar was unknown among the merudur.

The building was all on one level, either made of polished white stone or faced with it. The biggest panes of glass Adara had ever seen offered sweeping views of the Westwater while keeping out the elements. There was a rustic-looking barn and stables some distance from the cliff top and off to their left, and formal gardens of what appeared to be artfully-trained native seaside vegetation interspersed with stone walkways, fountains, and benches.

They headed for the stables, first. No one seemed to be around, and Lemas immediately set to removing their packs and the tack from the animals. There were six stalls, but only one of them was occupied at the moment. A tall, slender mare like an elongated version of Zarhya, with her dapple gray markings, poked her head out over the stall door and whickered at them curiously.

Adara hopped down to assist with the task. "Where is everybody?" she asked. Lemas hadn't really given her all that many details about his home and family.

"Nobody lives here but Father, Diurla, and my little brother Dresan," he told her. "We don't have any servants. There should be two more horses here, so probably two of them are off in Prizlion on business."

Adara stripped off Zarhya's saddle, then got out a rag and set about rubbing her down. She'd had an easy couple of days in a stable in Meruzal followed by a walk of no more than five miles to get from there to here, so she didn't really need it. "Would your parents leave your brother alone?" she asked, curious. She was still having trouble wrapping her head around the idea of people who took two hundred years to reach adulthood.

"Probably not," Lemas admitted. "We'll see after we get the animals dealt with and go inside." They put the horses and mule in the three empty stalls after forking in some straw, and left them with hay and water. By now Malika was quite used to putting up in barns, and she'd already flown up to the hayloft to take a nap after her late breakfast.

The eastern coast of Elyrion being only a couple of hundred miles west of Meruzal, there was little time difference. The sun was marginally less far above the eastern horizon here than it had been when they'd left, making it mid-morning. Adara and Lemas left Debardo's packs, which mostly contained their camping and archaeological gear, in the barn. But they took their personal packs along with them to the house.

The main entrance of the house sat beneath a stone portico, the door a massive thing carved out of a slab of some dark, iron-like wood. There were fantastic animals chasing each other around the perimeter, and a pair of long-necked, sharp-beaked birds with talons, facing each other as if in confrontation, in the center. Adara eyed them with interest.

"The crest of clan Azarion," Lemas said with a hint of pride. "The azar is a mythical bird, supposedly the size of an eagle but with a long neck and legs. Merudur myth claims they were impervious to heat, and it was an azar who befriended the founding member of my clan and brought her fire from the sun."

Adara smiled at that. It was good to know, somehow, that even people as ancient and wise as the merudur had some silly-ass myths. You scarcely needed magical birds bringing you fire from the sun, when every summer storm sparked a dozen forest fires.

The massive door was not locked, and Lemas pushed it open as if he lived there. Which he had, up until a few months ago. "Hello the house!" he called out cheerfully, "Anybody home?" There was a muffled shout from an area of the house off to their left, and Lemas set his pack down on a stone table that sat in the entry hall. "Just leave your things here," he told Adara. "Father's home!"

Adara felt a tightening in her midsection. She was an interloper here. She'd seduced the son of the house away from his duties as a smith's apprentice, drawn him into an ill-advised relationship, and shown up uninvited expecting to be granted hospitality and favors. What kind of a reaction was she going to get?

Clearly Lemas didn't share her misgivings. Was that just because he was young and naïve? They walked into a high-ceilinged room that had an enormous plate glass window offering a view to the northeast, with more of the western coast and a swath of gray sea. A merudur man who looked like a slimmer, bluer duplicate of Lemas, dressed in a long blue tunic and white trousers, was standing before an enormous easel on which a painting of a jungle full of tropical plants was in progress. The picture was astonishingly good, looking almost as if it might be a window into another world.

The man turned from his work at their approach, a palette in hand, and his eyes lit as he saw Lemas come in. He hastily set the palette down on a nearby taboret and clasped his son in a bear hug.

"Lemas! Where did *you* spring from? I thought you were in Carlienne!"

The young smith hugged his father back with every sign of deep affection. Two hundred years might be a short time in a lifespan of two millennia, Adara realized, but it was still a good long time in which to form a strong parent-child bond. The more so if you were likely to have only the one child. She held back hesitantly in the doorway, not wanting to intrude on their reunion.

Lemas broke away from the brace and smilingly gestured toward Adara. "I've come from Carlienne on a quest for the Sword of Myralis, Father!" he declared with enthusiasm. "I'd like you to meet Adara Willoughby. Adara, this is my father – Niemas of clan Azarion."

Adara watched anxiously as Niemas' large eyes, a little more blue than purple, widened at the sight of her and then shot to his son. The look he saw there told him all he needed to know, and he smiled broadly and held out a hand. "Delighted to meet you Miss Willoughby," he said with evident sincerity.

They had all been speaking in Franca, and it was clear Niemas had as good a command of that tongue as his son did. The painter turned back to his palette. "This is a wonderful surprise," he said. "Just let me put away my paints and we can go into the sitting room so you can tell me all about your quest."

While Adara watched in interest, Niemas produced a collection of small glass jars, each with a metal screw top, and began using a palette knife to scrape the blobs of paint from the polished wooden palette into the jars before capping each one tightly.

She knew nothing about painting, though she had met a couple of painters in the capital during her two months of hobnobbing with Carlienne's elite last year. The nobility loved having people with talent around them – artists, musicians, and entertainers – though of course those people were not quite of their own exalted social class. From what she'd seen in the drawing rooms of the high and mighty, Niemas' work was as good as anything being produced in Eorla. She wondered if he did portraiture, as well. That was where the big money was in painting, where she came from.

Soon Niemas had finished storing his paints in air-tight containers to keep them from drying out, and had cleaned his brushes and other equipment with a fluid that had a strong, pungent odor and reminded Adara of the pine woods near Nanny Selden's cottage.

He took off his blousy tunic, which Adara now realized was a smock worn over an intricately embroidered linen shirt. What a handsome man he was, she thought as he hung it on a peg on the wall and gestured for them to come with him into the sitting room they'd passed through earlier. Though he couldn't hold a candle to his son, of course. Lemas combined elven grace and beauty with a warm physicality usually lacking in the pureblood merudur she'd met. Still, it was easy to imagine Niemas winning the love of a human woman. And what a woman she must have been, for him to cleave to her even knowing she was doomed to die in so short a time.

Niemas acted the genial host, and brought mugs and a pot of freshly-brewed tea. The temperature in the house was comfortable, but warm beverages seemed more appealing than cold on this blustery day in early spring. The furniture in the sitting room was carved from the same hard, dark wood as the front door, but padded with silk cushions stuffed with goose down.

When they were all seated with their cups of tea, Niemas looked expectantly at his son, and Lemas launched into an explanation of the events that had led to their coming here. He fetched the jeweled sword and signet ring that had been buried with Queen Myralis from their luggage, and the painter's eyes widened. They widened still more when Lemas casually explained how they had arrived on the beach below the house not an hour ago, rather than having to spend days getting here by ship.

Adara rather wished he had not mentioned that, as she was anxious that knowledge of Fatiha Baba should not spread too far. But Lemas clearly loved and trusted his father. And it would have been awkward to explain their appearance here otherwise. It could easily be learned that they had *not* arrived on any ship docking in Prizlion.

"Where are Diurla and Dresan, Father?" Lemas asked.

"Spending the day in Prizlion," Niemas replied. "Shopping, visiting with friends, and so forth. She's informed me she's planning to cook us supper when they return. I hope setting another two places won't be a problem." From his tone, Diurla was not someone who liked surprises being sprung on her. And had Lemas said she had "no longer wanted to mother him" after the birth of Dresan? Adara's anxiety, which had completely subsided after Niemas' warm welcome, began to stir again.

"We have some food with us," Adara put in. "And I know how to cook. I can help out, if extra mouths are going to be any bother." Niemas made a gesture of dismissal.

"Don't worry about it dear," he said kindly. "I'm sure everything will be fine. So Lemas, what's your plan? Will you and Adara continue the quest for the sword?"

"I'm hoping to talk with Diurla about that," he replied. "Diurla," not "Mother," Adara noted – that worm of anxiety gnawing at her again. "We think Frasios might be able to point us in the direction of materials in the Royal Historical Archive that would give us some indications of what really happened to the sword after Queen Myralis' death. Clearly it wasn't buried with her, and the Guardian we killed spoke as if he knew where it had gone. For all we know, it might have been common knowledge back then and the records have just gotten buried over the millennia."

Niemas frowned in concentration. He was an artist, not a scholar. But his father and son were both smiths, and he had certainly heard of the legendary lost Prizal. It was only his astonishing talent as a painter that had allowed him to avoid being pressed into the smithing trade. Falodar was an artist in his way, too, and sorry as he was that his son had not chosen to follow in his footsteps, Niemas would have been wasted as a smith. The painter sighed, and shrugged. "I couldn't possibly say," he admitted. "No doubt when Diurla comes home you can discuss it with her. I'm sure she can arrange for you and Adara to visit the Archive. Um, Adara, did Lemas tell me you can read the ancient merudur runes?"

She smiled at him. "And speak the language well enough to be understood," she said in modern Merudur. He smiled back, and rose to his feet. "Let's get you settled in then, shall we?" he suggested. "I suppose once you find a lead to the sword you'll be haring off again?"

"Likely without the speed we used getting here," Adara said regretfully. "The necklace will only take us to someplace we've been before."

He nodded at that, and led them down a hall. Then he turned to face his guests. "Um, Lemas, I suppose you could bunk in Dresan's room, and Adara could have your old room… I know he'd be delighted to share it with you."

"Father, Adara is my consort," Lemas said seriously. "We will sleep together in my old bed."

A look of fleeting pain crossed Niemas' beautiful features as he heard his son's words. He'd known it just from looking at them, but he had hoped otherwise. Whether or not Adara intended to spend her life with Lemas and bear his children, the boy was in love with her and hurt would come soon or late. He sighed. There was nothing to be done about it.

"Ah," he said quietly. "Very well. You know the way, son. I'll leave you to get settled." He handed over Adara's pack, which he'd been carrying, and walked back down the hall. Adara glared at Lemas.

"Why did you tell him that?" she hissed. His face fell, and she immediately felt bad for taking him to task. But she had *warned* him from the start that she was not going to be "his"!

"I'm sorry," he said softly, leaning forward to put a hand on her shoulder. "I just… I just want to be together with you, not spending the night longing for you while you're just across the hall." Adara stood on tiptoe and planted a sweet kiss on his mouth.

Then she said matter-of-factly, "Sleeping together in a house full of people is likely to put a damper on our sex life anyhow. You know that, right?" He grinned.

"We'll see," he said, and pushed open the door of his childhood bedroom.

# Chapter 15

By the time Diurla and Dresan returned from their day of shopping and visiting in the capital, Niemas had gone back to his painting. The rain had stopped, and after a light lunch Lemas had taken Adara on a tour of the house and grounds. Climate aside, it was as beautiful as she'd always imagined Elyrion to be.

Malika had accompanied them, trotting along beside them or taking to the air. She seemed overjoyed with the fishing opportunities in the little cove beneath the bluff, and had caught and eaten two more good-sized fish before deciding she would like to go back to the hayloft for another nap.

Adara and Lemas were visiting with the animals when they heard the clopping of hooves and saw a pair of riders approaching on tall horses like the one they'd found in the stables on their arrival. The smaller figure shouted "Lemas!" and put his heels to his mount, dashing up to them and then leaping from the saddle and into Lemas' arms.

Grinning from ear to ear, Lemas hugged his little brother. No so little as all that, Adara realized. She had envisioned a child, but Dresan stood well over five feet tall and was probably close to reaching adolescence. He was a beautiful boy, resembling his father in facial features but with a slightly bluish cast to his long silken hair. He wore it tied back in a ponytail, and was dressed in linen shirt and trousers beneath a waterproof cloak.

The other rider came up to them, one of the most beautiful women Adara had ever seen. As she dismounted, Adara realized she was scarcely any taller than she herself was – a couple of inches under six feet. That made her "petite" as merudur woman went. Her long, flowing hair was a pale blue color, her tip-tilted eyes enormous and a limpid blue-violet, with thick indigo lashes. She eyed Adara with a frozen expression on her face, neither smiling nor scowling, before turning to Lemas.

"You're here," she said in a mellifluous voice, her tone utterly neutral.

"Hello, Diurla," Lemas said. His tone was friendly enough, but it was certainly not a greeting to a woman who'd stood in as his mother since he was a child. They did not embrace.

"And who is this?" the merudur woman asked, with a nod toward Adara.

Lemas smiled. He'd had decades to get used to coldness from his father's consort, after all. "Diurla of the clan Cabrilion, this is my consort Adara Willoughby. Adara, my stepmother. And this is my brother Dresan, of the clan Azarion." Adara put on a smile and extended her hand. Diurla touched it limply, Dresan clasped it firmly – eyeing her with a look that suggested adolescence wasn't all that far away. Did elves ever get spotty, she wondered idly?

"So nice to meet both of you," Adara said politely. "I'm curious, do merudur children automatically belong to their father's clan?"

"No," Diurla replied shortly. "Male children join their father's clan, female children their mother's. It mostly balances out, though certainly some clans are larger than others."

Adara felt glad to have gotten that much out of the woman. She had a sense that Lemas' return to the family household was *not* welcome as far as Diurla was concerned, and that his bringing along a human woman and claiming her as a consort met with even less approval.

She decided to pretend everything was fine. "We've been here since this morning, and had a nice lunch with Niemas," Adara said cheerfully. "We were just getting ready to go into the house. Can I help carry in your packages?" There were quite a few bundles tied to the horses' saddles.

"I'll get it," Lemas volunteered. He, too, appeared determined to remain cheerful in the face of his stepmother's frosty reception. He took down the various bundles from the horses and then he and Dresan set about unsaddling them.

"I'll rub them down, Lemas," the boy said. "It's my job." His big brother gave him a friendly slap on the shoulder, then lifted the packages all in one load and the three of them moved toward the front door.

Diurla led the way inside and called out in Merudur, "Niemas, we're home! Might I have a word with you?" Adara exchanged glances with Lemas. It seemed better to avoid pissing off the lady of the house any more than she already was, by letting her say something that was going to embarrass her.

"We're only here in Elyrion for a few days, Diurla," Adara said in Merudur.

The woman turned and stared at her, eyes widening. Then she nodded. "A pity you can't stay longer, dear," she replied in the same language, fairly dripping insincerity. Diurla declined Adara's offers of food and kitchen assistance, so the four of them – Adara and the Azarion men – retired to the sitting room to relax with snacks and drinks as they waited for the food to be prepared.

Of course the entire story of the quest for the Sword of Myralis had to be retold for the benefit of young Dresan, who unsurprisingly (since he clearly idolized his older brother) thought it was the most amazing and wonderful thing he had ever heard of. Recalling her own brother's similar attitude last year, which had led to him inviting himself along on the quest for the tomb of the kobold king and nearly getting himself killed, Adara made sure to play up the dangers and hardships while downplaying the rewards.

"Naturally, once we find the sword, we'll be turning it over to the Royal Historical Archive," she told the boy. "I have no need of treasure, but it's fitting that the merudur people should have this important artifact returned to them so all will have a chance to see it."

Dresan handled the jeweled sword they'd brought from Myralis' tomb, awe in his expression. Lemas might have found it tackily over-decorated, but to a boy Dresan's age it seemed the very epitome of a legendary royal blade. It actually was probably a serviceable-enough weapon – the edge was sharp, and perfectly preserved by the same spell that had kept its owner looking freshly dead for nine thousand years. But all those gems made it a little too heavy at the hilt, and hard to grip. Adara would rather have Voleur in her hands than this thing, if it came to a fight.

Dinner was served as night was falling, on an elegant table carved from the same wood as the sitting room furnishings. It only seated eight, and Adara guessed that out here so far from the capital Niemas and his consort must not often entertain.

Diurla had outdone herself, or so Niemas proclaimed. Adara had no standards for comparison of the merudur matron's usual culinary productions, but the food was excellent. And there was enough of it, the addition of one very large, very hungry young smith notwithstanding. Despite their seaside location it was not seafood for a change, but rather roasted leg of lamb with a red wine and mushroom sauce, asparagus tips sautéed in butter, and a colorful pilaf made with some kind of grain. They washed it down with bottles of a dry red produced in Elyrion. Dresan had his with water added.

The tale of the quest for Prizal was repeated yet again, this time (with enthusiasm) by Dresan. Diurla cocked an eyebrow, surprised at the information. She had never imagined her stepson as the adventurous sort, though many young merudur men might seek adventure during an early stage of their lives. And the young human woman who spoke passable Merudur, and claimed to be able to read the ancient runes, was something of a puzzle. Though as tall and slender as an elf, she looked scarcely old enough to be out on her own.

Adara touched on some of her other adventures for the benefit of Lemas' family, often at his urging. He was proud of her, she realized, and she found it touching. Finally, as they were finishing up a dessert of pastry folded around whipped cream and preserved summer berries, she broached the reason for their visit.

"Lemas suggested that we should consult with you, Diurla," Adara said. She felt that the tension between her and her hostess had eased somewhat during the evening. "I understand you have a friend, Frasios of clan Berandion, who works at the Royal Historical Archive?"

"That's right," Diurla responded. "He and I were together for a few decades – long before I met Niemas, of course. No children came of our union, but we've remained friends."

"Back in Carlienne," Adara explained, "I went through all of the ancient merudur historical documents that were confiscated from Meruzal at the conclusion of the Elvany War. I found a reference to the burial of Queen Myralis and the merudur dead from the war with the pinudur, but there was no actual mention of the sword Prizal.

That, as we found when we uncovered Myralis' resting place, had not been interred with her. We're hoping that your friend Frasios might have some information that was not contained in the Meruzal archives, or could point us to a section of the archives in Prizlion where we might search for references to the sword."

Diurla considered for a moment, musing. "It's very possible that there might be something in the Royal Historical Archive that was not in Meruzal," she said. "As you undoubtedly know, when the merudur were eventually forced to retreat from the continent, most of the government's records were carried with them to Prizlion."

"That's what I suspected," Adara replied.

"I tell you what," Diurla went on, "you young people can relax tomorrow and I'll go into the capital again and confer with Frasios. Who knows, perhaps he has some information at his fingertips. In any case, I can arrange for him to give you some time in the near future, or get permission for you to search the archives. They are of course not opened to just anyone, and Frasios' time is valuable. For the sake of our friendship, though, I think I can get him to help you."

Dresan had been sent to bed a bit ahead of the adults, Adara and Lemas not turning in until their host and hostess excused themselves. Lemas childhood bedroom was a good-sized chamber, with an intricately patterned wool carpet covering the stone floor and a bed that was about as wide as a normal "double" inn bed in Tanar but considerably longer. The young elf's feet had been hanging over the end of all of the beds he and Adara had shared since they'd been traveling together.

The walls of the chamber, like the walls throughout the house, were hung with Niemas' paintings. He did indeed do portraits, surprisingly filled with warm light though the subjects were usually cool, pale, and bluish. "Father's been famous throughout Elyrion since long before I was born," Lemas told Adara. "Neither my mother nor Diurla ever needed to work at anything outside the home, thanks to the income from his art."

Adara began removing her clothing, walking around and looking at the room's contents as she tried to imagine the elf lad who had grown up here. In among what was probably a king's ransom in original artworks were souvenirs: a broken spear Lemas said he'd found washed up on the beach in the cove; a collection of seashells; an iron dagger that had been his first successful effort at smithing.

Lemas remained standing there, watching his lover with a bemused expression as she strolled against the backdrop of these familiar objects. He actually had a beautiful woman, here in the room where he'd grown up – where he'd masturbated countless times as he dreamed that someone like her would come into his life. He wished more than anything that she truly *were* his consort, and that she was elven or had some magical power that would prolong her life so he would never have to lose her. But he knew it was not to be. They had now, and that would have to be enough for them.

When she was down to her underwear he stepped to her side, enfolding her a tight embrace and locking his mouth on hers in a deep kiss. "You can't imagine what a turn-on it is, having you here in this room!" he murmured. Adara looked up at him questioningly. Having never been an adolescent boy, she had no idea what he was talking about. She herself was feeling constrained, an interloper in this house shacking up with the elder son. It was hard to believe she really had permission to be here, let alone do all the things with Lemas that she so enjoyed doing.

"You naughty boy," Adara said under her breath, kissing him and rubbing against the front of his trousers. That gigantic cock was on the rise again. As she thought about it, it *was* kind of a turn-on, the whole forbidden aspect. They were both adults, and they weren't trying to hide anything. But it still felt as if they were sneaking around somehow, engaging in guilty pleasures.

Adara pulled her camisole up over her head, letting her breasts bounce free, and then stepped out of her drawers to stand naked before him. "Well," she murmured, looking up at her elven lover with mischief in her eyes, "are you planning to participate?"

His eyes alight with desire, Lemas very quickly got out of his clothing. Then he drew her into his arms again. He loved the feel of skin on skin, Adara's somehow always warmer than his own. He put his hand down to her crotch and inserted two fingers between her nether lips, feeling the moisture there. It appeared he and she were of like minds.

He wanted very much just to throw her down on that virginal childhood bed of his and pierce her with his throbbing cock. But Adara had taught him quite a few things in their time together, and he knew it would be more enjoyable for her if he took his time.

Lemas scooped Adara up off the floor, gathering her in his arms, and carried her over to lay her down on the bed near the foot. Then he knelt on the floor in front of her, and gently spread her thighs apart so he could reach her moist crevice with his mouth. She let out a quiet sigh with a little shudder at the end of it, and humped her mound up into his face.

Adara lay on her back with her legs spread, as Lemas worked her over with his lips, tongue, and fingers. One advantage of having an elf for a lover, she thought – no beard, and no razor stubble. That women also pleasured other women in this way was something she was completely unaware of. Same-sex love was never spoken of in the society of Tanar.

She closed her eyes, giving herself over to the warm wet sensations and letting her mind drift. Soon she was pressing down hard on the mattress, digging into it with her fingers, as she felt an orgasm coming on. Must… not… scream… "Aah, Ahhhh!" Adara moaned, stifling the urge to cry out loudly as she usually did. Somehow that only excited her more, and she bucked wildly beneath Lemas' mouth before collapsing in a boneless heap.

Grinning and wiping his mouth with his hand, Lemas crawled up onto the bed beside her and held her close, covering her face, her shoulders, her breasts with tender kisses. His erection, degrees warmer than the rest of him, throbbed between their bodies. Then he pulled away a little, and helped Adara sit up. He bent close and murmured in her ear, "Why don't you kneel facing the headboard?"

Another warm rush swept through Adara at that suggestion. She'd had a fondness for this position ever since Ferdyn had introduced her to it in similar circumstances – making love in secret in one of the bedrooms at his family's house in King's Crossing. That house had never been his childhood home, however. Were she and Lemas acting out some lubricious fantasy from his adolescence, she wondered?

Adara knelt before Lemas on the bed, and he knelt behind her – carefully inserting the tip of his pulsating member into her juice-glistening orifice. Ohhh, yes… As she engulfed him, he fought a momentary urge to shoot on the spot. She'd had no complaints about the duration of his second and third efforts, but he still felt as though coming too fast the first time was failing to uphold some imaginary standard. He knew she'd had other lovers, men at a later stage of life than he was. His goal was to become her best, the man she would remember forever – even if they were not to be together long term, even if other lovers would follow him.

Lemas began stroking slowly, going in deep and coming almost all the way back out again, as the excitement built. Adara was trying not to make noise, with Dresan's room just across the hall, and that was making it hard for him to tell how he was doing, whether she was close to coming again. But he soon realized that while she was not moaning and crying out as she usually did, he could tell a lot from the sound of her breathing.

He gripped one of her nicely rounded, muscular butt cheeks in each hand, thrusting harder and faster as he felt Adara's response building. They had been at this for no more than a couple of minutes when he felt his control slipping away. But from her strangled moans, it was time. As he pounded into her, sinking his shaft to the fullest, he felt her vaginal walls clasp him in rhythmic waves. She was coming, and so was he!

Much later, after the second time, they lay snuggled together talking quietly before drifting into sleep. "I have to admit, I had a lot of orgasms in this room before those two," Lemas said. "But those two were by far the best." Adara snorted and reached down to squeeze his now definitely flaccid member.

"So you've realized your boyhood dreams?" she asked, amused.

"You might say that," he admitted. "Some of them, anyway. I still have to find the Sword of Myralis, receive the accolades of the grateful merudur nation, and carve my name on the annals of history."

"Tomorrow," Adara suggested sleepily, kissing him on the right nipple before rolling over and closing her eyes.

# *Chapter 16*

They were all up early except Niemas, who tended to keep artist's hours. Adara supposed that anyone with his astonishing ability was fully entitled to sleep as late as he wanted to. She quite liked Lemas' father, and his younger brother seemed to be a sweet kid. Diurla, she was trying to like. But it was a bit of a challenge. Eh, it was not as if she was marrying into his family or anything like that. She felt a pang as she suddenly recalled that this loving idyll she'd been enjoying would soon enough come to an end.

Everyone was expected to get their own breakfast, it seemed, but there was plenty of food on hand. The kitchen was unlike anything Adara had seen before, a room to itself with a bronze free-standing stove in the middle of it. It was fueled not by wood but by oil – the same oil that was used to light lamps throughout Niemas' home.

There were stone countertops providing plenty of space for food preparation, and a metal chest set into them on one side that, when Adara opened it, proved to be nearly thirty degrees cooler inside than the ambient temperature. "Lemas, what *is* this?" Adara demanded in amazement.

"Just a cold chest," he replied, as if such things were common as dirt.

"But how…?"

He grinned at her. "It's enchanted," he admitted. "It's been in our family for centuries. He gestured to a palm-sized gem mounted in the chest's lid. "The gem draws energy, sucking heat out of the surrounding air," he explained. "If it ever got hot here, which it doesn't, we could take the gem out of the chest and use it to cool the house, probably."

Adara's mind was immediately engaged. "But… then, why doesn't everything in the chest freeze solid? Shouldn't the gem just keep gobbling heat until there was none left?"

"I hadn't thought about that," Lemas admitted. "I think the enchantment is set so that it's only hungry for temperatures a little above freezing. At least, nothing we've kept in it has ever frozen. You'd have to ask the enchanter, I suppose."

"And could I?" Adara asked. Hanging around with the merudur was giving her a warped perspective on time, she realized. You want to know what happened a few hundred years ago? Just go find the witnesses and ask them. "Um, truthfully I'm not sure," Lemas responded. "Father would probably know."

After breakfast Dresan was eager to take them on yet another tour of the neighborhood, as Diurla set off for Prizlion and a consultation with her old friend; and Niemas emerged from his bedchamber, yawning, and went looking for something to eat. He would likely spend most of the day completing the painting that had been on his easel when they arrived.

Adara, Lemas, and Dresan mounted up and rode off along the bluff in the direction of the next house at around mid-morning. Dresan had been utterly enchanted to meet Malika, having neither seen such a creature before nor dreamed they might exist. He seemed to be nearly as infatuated with the semigryph as Ferdyn had been, and she happily accepted his devotion. Adara wondered idly if she'd created a monster – a flying predator who'd discovered how to use cuteness to manipulate people.

Prizlion stood a little over five miles north of Niemas' house, and it took Diurla less than a full hour to reach the royal palace complex. She tied her mount to one of the hitching posts that had been provided in the central courtyard, which offered access to a dozen royal departments. The merudur had had many millennia in which to perfect bureaucracy, and they had done well with it.

As she glided in through the door leading to the Royal Historical Archive's wing, she was greeted by a receptionist and passed through immediately. She had been here often. Diurla pushed through the door to Frasios' offices without bothering to knock. The scholar, as usual, was working at a large stone table in the anteroom, which gave on corridors stacked high with records. He appeared to be restoring an ancient scroll.

Her beautiful eyes lit as she came into the room on her soft shoes, making no sound. Dear Frasios, how distracted the man could be! As he concentrated on what he was doing, she slipped past him and then wrapped her arms around his midsection from behind. The elf nearly jumped out of his voluminous, pale blue robes.

"Diurla!" he exclaimed, on discovering who it was. "Back so soon?"

"You know I can't stay away from you," she purred. Frasios sighed. Among a race of tall, beautiful people, he was a few inches shorter than most and had had the astonishing misfortune to begin losing his hair when he was no more than three hundred years old.

Diurla claimed that she had fallen in love with him for his mind, and that mind was still in perfect condition. Yet they had never made a child together – usually an indication that the female partner in the relationship was not sufficiently inspired. Only real love could release the hormones that would allow a merudur woman to ovulate, and even when she did the chances of conception were not great.

He sighed again. His former consort was the most beautiful woman Frasios had ever known, and she still thrilled him to the core whenever they met. And she claimed she loved him still, had "proven" it by having sex with him on numerous occasions. But it had been that artist Niemas to whom she had borne a son, not him. He just didn't know what to make of her, but felt helpless to deny her anything when she made her occasional appearances in his life. Only yesterday she had come here, wanting some little favor. Would he look into the archives and see whether the lineage of clan Azarion included any famous magi?

Diurla drew him to her and kissed him full on the lips, sending a thrill though Frasios and temporarily short-circuiting his mind. She had been his first and only consort, and the way things were going it was beginning to look as though a life devoted to scholarship would be his slim compensation for never having a family, never finding lasting love. Yet, if she were not truly drawn to him, why did she keep coming back?

Frasios broke the embrace and took a step backward. He was not, he hoped, a complete idiot. "What do you want, Diurla?" he asked. "Why are you here?"

"I can't just be here because I miss you, Frasi?" she crooned, using the pet name that had driven him wild when they'd been together.

He gathered his resolve. "Not that I've noticed, no," he said stiffly. Diurla sized him up, and concluded it was time to cut through the bull.

"My lummox of a stepson showed up yesterday," she said in tones of malice. "With, if you can believe it, some human bimbo he picked up in Carlienne!" Frasios looked at her in puzzlement. He knew Diurla was not fond of her consort's elder son, and had maneuvered to have him packed off to apprentice with his grandfather on the continent. But what did this have to do with *him*?

Diurla realized that details would be required, and provided them. "They're searching for the Sword of Myralis," she explained. "Lemas' whore actually figured out how to find the queen's tomb in Elvany, and learned that Prizal was not interred with her. Now they're here wanting to search the Royal Historical Archives for any mentions of it. It's an obsession with smiths, you know."

Frasios *didn't* know, but he was willing to take her word. The eons of merudur history offered many, many non-sword-related episodes, and while he'd heard of Prizal it didn't loom nearly as large in his consciousness as it did with Falodar and his ilk.

He shrugged. "What do you want *me* to do about it?" he asked. Diurla took him by the arm and led him away from the work table, her hip pressed against his. She guided him to a padded bench against one wall of the space, and pulled him down to sit beside her.

"I want them out of Prizlion, out of Elyrion, as quickly as possible," she said. "Lemas is well set with his grandfather in Carlienne. He needs none of Niemas' possessions. Everything should rightfully be the property of Dresan, and I am determined that it *will* be. Niemas' insane penchant for humans has made him the ancestor of gods-know how many inferior little humans on the continent. But Dresan is his only pureblood child, and his rightful heir."

Frasios blinked. Niemas was somewhat notorious for having taken a human woman as consort and fathered three children on her, a scandalously large number of offspring among the merudur. Two of them were long dead, of course, and their human descendants in Tanar were of no import among the merudur. But Lemas... Well, he could understand why Diurla was so protective of her chick. He kind of wished Dresan were *their* chick, but how could he deny her whatever she wanted?

"You want me to send them off on a wild goose chase, get them away from Elyrion?" Frasios asked. Diurla nodded.

"Better still if it's a goose chase that might get them killed," she said. "I don't need the seed of Niemas producing another line of humans to cloud its legacy. As far as I'm concerned Dresan is the only legitimate heir of Niemas' branch of clan Azarion."

Frasios pondered. He had spent most of every day of his working life studying, cataloging, filing, and preserving the written records of the merudur nation. They went back far beyond Queen Myralis, starting as primitive tribes on Elyrion before learning the mariners' art and spilling out onto the nearby continent. And his memory was excellent. It was one of the reasons he'd been drawn to this work.

"I have an idea," he said at last. "There are only fragmentary records of Prizal from the time after Myralis, nothing that could pinpoint the location. But I can put your stepson and his human consort on a path that should send them flying from these shores." After he had explained what he had in mind, Diurla kissed him deeply. Then she unbuttoned his trousers.

# Chapter 17

In the morning after breakfast Lemas and Adara saddled Sadiq and Zarhya for the ride into Prizlion. Lemas had accompanied his stepmother on visits to Frasios a time or two in his younger days, and was able to guide them easily. Adara was in awe as they drew within the city limits. Prizlion was not the sprawling stew of humanity that Carlienne was, but it had a pristine beauty. It was like the difference between a mountain meadow rampant in spring, and an exquisitely manicured garden. One that had been tended for eons.

"Was Prizlion always the capital of the merudur nation?" Adara asked Lemas as they found themselves leaving the dirt path to trot along well-tended stone-paved streets.

"Before the merudur spread to Eorla," he said, "the capital of Elyrion was at Mercasel on the western coast. After my ancestors had become a sea power, and established their kingdom of Silaine, it was moved to Meruzal. Prizlion was built on the site of a fishing village to become the new capital after the merudur were driven back to Elyrion."

Adara mused on that. The merudur had fallen far from their former glory. Yet despite being outnumbered by humans, they maintained a vibrant society with much to offer the world. She hoped future ages would not see conflict between humans and elves that would result in elves being driven to extinction. Then she had a strange thought.

"Lemas," Adara said, "I don't know whether you're aware of this, but there's a phenomenon among the humans of Eorla that might have some bearing on your family. Have you ever heard of 'changelings'?"

"Can't say that I have," he replied, as they wended their way through crowded streets toward the royal complex.

"Sometimes," Adara went on, "A human man and woman may have a baby who at first appears normal. But in the first few months, differences become apparent. The child does not develop as quickly as it should, and its features begin to appear elven – the pointed ears, the big eyes, skin that's not the same color as that of its parents."

"A secret elven lover?" Lemas suggested. While a child's mother could never be in doubt, fatherhood was another thing entirely.

"No, I don't think so," Adara replied. "Folklore has it that the elves steal human children and replace them with babies of their own, for some nefarious purpose that's never truly defined. It's absurd – any human parents with an elven baby to raise would die of old age before their little one had reached adolescence. Right?"

Lemas nodded. His human mother had aged and died while he was still a young child. He looked at Adara, wondering where she was going with this. "What if," she went on, "what if the elven part of a half-elven child's heritage is hidden, when they appear to be fully human, but still present? What if your human siblings, who returned to Eorla after they had grown up, still carried within them the possibility of producing an elven child?"

He wrestled with that idea. It was clear that children carried the characteristics of their parents, but for people like him there was a sharp divide. His full siblings, long since dead of old age, had shared the same parents but had appeared to be fully human. Just as he appeared to be fully an elf, if a little more robust and ruddy-complected than most of the merudur.

"So you're saying these changelings are actually full elves, having received a hidden elven heritage from both their apparently human but actually part-elven parents?" Lemas asked. He was flabbergasted at the thought.

"Exactly," Adara said. "Since you said that three out of four children of an elf-human liaison would appear fully human, I think that the human heritage must somehow dominate the elven. Yet even if those human children don't express their elven heritage, it may be in their blood – ready to come out again in future generations if they mate with another who has that blood."

Lemas' mind reeled. Did that mean…? "So if the human heritage is dominant, how can I possess the elven form and lifespan – despite my differences in build and coloring?"

"I think your mother must have had a hidden elven heritage," Adara responded immediately. "It may be more complicated than 'elf/not elf,' but I think that you are actually, in everything that matters, a full elf. Not really a half-blood. It's your human siblings who were half-bloods, and some of their descendants might end up being full elves."

Gods, what a thought! But he sensed that Adara was on the right track. They arrived at the royal compound, and hitched their horses in the central courtyard. It was time to put aside this fascinating line of reasoning and learn what, if anything, Frasios Berandion might be able to offer them in their hunt for the Sword of Myralis.

Frasios had instructed the receptionist to expect them, and they were let in immediately and followed a corridor to the section of the Archive where the scholar spent his days. He greeted them cordially. "Lemas, so good to see you!" he effused. "Are you sure you are fully adult? I swear you have grown since you were last here only a year or so ago!"

Lemas grinned. "Probably the muscle from working at Grandfather's forge," he said. "My old master didn't work me half as hard. Frasios, I'd like you to meet my consort Adara Willoughby. As Diurla told you, Adara and I are on the hunt for information about the final resting place of Prizal. What can you tell us?"

Adara thought Lemas had gotten to the point rather quickly. Was this Frasios not as dear a family friend as all that? He certainly was the oddest-looking member of the merudur she had ever seen – scarcely taller than herself, and mostly bald with only a slight fringe of pale hair hanging lankly to his shoulders. She had no trouble at all picturing him as a man who spend his days immersed in books, with few opportunities for contact with other people.

She had a great deal more trouble picturing the beautiful Diurla having chosen to shack up with this unlikely-looking specimen. Niemas was tall and gorgeous, and a wonderful artist as well. But what might she have seen in Frasios? One of the frustrating things about hanging out with the merudur, Adara was finding, was the inability to tell how old someone was without asking them. A few hundred years might mean nothing to one of the udur, But the difference between five hundred and a thousand must surely reflect many formative experiences. Ah well…

After pressing the flesh Adara thought she ought to get right to the point, as well. "Can you direct us to the section of the archives where we might find information about Prizal, merun Berandion?" The nebbishy-looking archivist shook his head.

"I fear," he said, "that the archives contain no such information," he told her.

He went on, "The majority of what we have stored here dates from after the fall of Silaine. I have of course read every single item in the history section of the Archive over the past few hundred years, and I would certainly recall any mentions of Prizal. There was only one reference, a writer from around the time of the fall lamenting that the merudur no longer had that famous sword. He was convinced that had we still possessed it, we could have prevented the humans from driving us from the continent."

Adara's face fell. All this way for nothing? Well, not nothing really. She had gotten to meet Lemas' family, and see something of the fabled isle of the elves. It was definitely worth the trip for that, especially since they had not had to spend two gut-wrenching days and nights getting here by ship.

"Ah," Frasios put in when he saw her expression, "I do have *something* for you, however. Have you ever heard of Melandurin?" Adara drew a blank. There'd been no mention of a person by that name in any of the merudur historical documents she'd studied.

"Was he from the time of Queen Myralis?" she asked.

"Not at all," Frasios chuckled, amused at her wrong guess. "He is from our own time, indeed should now be little more than twelve hundred years old. Still a vigorous man, I would assume, though no one in Prizlion has seen him in many centuries." Feeling that she was being played with, Adara declined further comment as she waited for the archivist to explain himself.

Lemas had no such reservations, however. "I haven't heard of him either," he said. "Is he a historian?"

"I suppose that in a way you might call him that," Frasios said, a slight smile still playing about his lips. "He's a necromancer."

# Chapter 18

The sixty-foot schooner *Flissanda* bore west, coming around the ominously-named Barrow Island on its southern side. Adara and Lemas were gathering their packs, preparing to climb into the boat that would shortly be lowered over the side.

It had taken a day, a night, and part of another day for the little ship Adara had hired to reach this point a hundred miles south of Elyrion and somewhat further west – a lonely rock no more than five miles across sitting off the western coast of Eorla. Her merudur captain and crew were not happy to be coming here, but the pay had been more than they could resist. That, and Adara's promise that they would not have to stay near this place of treacherous currents and evil repute any longer than the time it would take to put their passengers ashore.

High cliffs ringed the island except for here on its western side, where a narrow tongue of clear water gave onto a shingle beach no more than twenty paces wide. It barely counted as a smuggler's cove, let alone a harbor. As the captain called for the sails to be slackened and the boat to be lowered, they came to the rail and looked shoreward. Had this really been such a good idea?

But according to Frasios, consulting with the necromancer might be their only hope for finding the lost sword. If he could call up the spirit of Myralis, she might be able to tell them what they needed to know. And they had come too far on this quest to give up now! Their horses and mule awaited their return at a commercial stable in Prizlion, a location Fatiha Baba stood ready to open to them at Adara's command.

Adara and then Lemas went down a rope ladder to the boat, their packs making it all the harder to negotiate the climb as ship and boat bucked and heaved on the breast of the Sunset Sea. Thank the gods today was a relatively calm day, Adara thought. The elven anti-seasickness potion had worked well for her, and she'd had no more than the slightest nausea during their journey. But still, the thought of all that water beneath them – dark and turbid and teeming with who-knows-what monsters – filled her with uneasiness. She was most anxious *not* to be going for a dip.

Adara and Lemas sat near the bow of the twelve-foot dinghy, as two of the ship's crewmen each took an oar and began pulling toward shore. As soon as Adara had sent a mental image to Malika of their plans, the semigryph had launched herself skyward and flown toward the beach. She was waiting on the strand, chewing on a freshly-caught fish, by the time the bottom scraped on the shingle and they hopped out of the boat.

"Thank you," Adara called in Merudur, and waved to the crewmen. They were already pulling away, anxious to leave Barrow Island behind. Their late passengers hurried up the slope to get away from the booming surf, then stood looking at a narrow path winding up beside a ravine where a small stream came down from the island's heights to spill into the sea.

There must be fresh water here, Adara realized, else how could this Melandurin have lived here for all these centuries? As it was, she had to wonder what he ate. There was grass and some heath vegetation on the island's slopes, but it didn't look like a good location for farming. Maybe he lived on fish and the eggs of sea birds? There were many of the latter nesting on the cliffs.

Malika's fish had been rather small, and she was already licking herself clean. Go see what's up there, Adara suggested silently, and she took to the air again. In the wild, semigryphs usually hunted like owls – haunting the nighttime woods and ghosting out on silent wings to pounce on unsuspecting prey. They were bigger than any owl in Eorla, though, and took animals far larger than mice. But Malika, raised from a half-grown kit by Adara and bonded with her mentally, had ideas her wild kin had probably never considered.

As Adara and Lemas stood at the foot of the trail, she rode along with the semigryph and looked out through her eyes. At the island's center there was a rocky peak, broken and weathered by the sea winds into a softly rounded shape. That sloped steeply down on all sides, then gave out onto a gently sloping plain that terminated abruptly in the cliffs.

At Adara's suggestion Malika flew higher, soaring on the fresh breeze, and drew nearer to the peak – searching with her raptor's eyes for any signs of human habitation. There! A short distance from the top, on the same side of the island as the little cove, was a structure that resembled an ancient hill fort, or one of the mountain castles warlords in the part of Eorla now controlled by Tanar used to build for themselves. A few of those still stood, though most had fallen into disuse since Unification. It looked as if it had been carved out of the rock itself.

"Looks like it's going to be a long walk, followed by a steep climb," Adara told Lemas. "I suppose we'd better get going." Just then she got a powerful sending from Malika: Terror! An image of a hideous black visage, eyes and mouth windows onto a sheet of flames, came through the mental bond. Adara felt a jolt of panic herself. Come, she commanded, and in seconds the semigryph was overhead and coming down for a landing. She dove into Adara's arms, nearly knocking her down. Now nearing full adulthood, Malika weighed close to thirty pounds.

"Oof! There, there, it's all right…" Adara snugged Malika to her and stroked her fur, scratching behind the ears, and felt the fear subside. In another few moments she was able to let the heavy creature down to the ground. Lemas was eyeing the pair of them questioningly.

"She took fright at something," Adara explained, mind working hard as she tried to analyze what had happened. "She was soaring up toward the peak, where the necromancer's holdfast is located, and then suddenly she was scared out of her wits. It has to have been a magical sending."

"Hmm," Lemas responded. "I suppose it's possible that an ancient practitioner of dark magical arts who makes his home on a remote island might not be all that receptive to uninvited guests."

Adara grinned. "You think? But I hadn't actually expected him to attack a harmless animal." Calling Malika "harmless" was a bit inaccurate, but she hadn't been storming his fortress or anything, just flying around on a bit of reconnaissance.

Sighing, Adara said "I think you two had better stay here for now. I'll go beard the old bastard in his den. His magical attacks won't work on me, but I think Sierlas might work on *him*."

"Uh, try not to kill him too much?" Lemas replied. "Don't forget we need his help."

She grinned at him wolfishly. "Keep down below the cliff top," Adara admonished. "If Malika starts acting like she wants you to come after me, it'll be because I sent for her." She set off up the trail beside the ravine at a quick pace. Moments after she reached the top of the cliffs and put her feet on the trail leading toward the fortress, she felt the Darkshield pulse.

I wonder what spell that was, Adara mused as she hiked along. Whatever it had been, she soon felt others come. None of them, of course, would have any effect on her while she wore the Darkshield. Old Melandurin must be crapping his magus robes by now, she thought, as she crossed the sloping plain and began climbing up into the rocks. He probably thinks I'm some powerful magus come to take over.

She kind of wished she *was*. Since it seemed she had a natural aptitude for some forms of magic, perhaps she ought to seek out a master. Her Learning Ring should make learning magic as easy as any of the other pursuits she'd mastered since obtaining it.

It had taken no more than half an hour to cross the plain, but the trail became steep and rocky as Adara climbed toward the fortress in the rocks above. Soon she was puffing, and wishing she were wearing mountaineering boots instead of the soft, sturdy ones she usually wore for traveling. A walking stick of some kind would be nice, too, but she wasn't about to use Sierlas for such a purpose.

Catching her breath, Adara peered upward. The rocky tor at the island's center was surely no more than two thousand feet above the surface of the sea below the cliffs; but it seemed much higher now she was climbing it. As the trail wound its way upward, she kept losing sight of the fortress and then seeing it again – growing ever closer.

Details that Malika hadn't picked up were becoming visible, now. It wasn't really a fortress – almost more of a cliff dwelling. There were a few sites in Eorla where the early human immigrants from Frigan had settled, taking advantage of natural limestone caves and enlarging them to create cliffside complexes safe from the continent's large land-bound predators. There was definitely a tower, a circular thing that appeared to be made of the same stone as the tor itself. But whether it had actually been carved from the rock, Adara could not tell.

The magical attacks had ceased. Adara went through a narrow defile, a small creek flowing in a ravine to her right and scrubby trees barely finding purchase amid the rocks on either side of the trail. Then she rounded a bend, and found herself standing on a flat, sandy space maybe thirty feet from side to side and fifty between the end of the winding trail and the fortress pressed up against the cliffside ahead. There were no ground floor windows, and just a single heavy wooden door leading inside.

That door stood open, and between it and Adara stood a tall merudur man in deep blue robes. He held a wooden staff with a glowing crystal mounted in the end, and his face bore a look of puzzlement and apprehension. "A human woman!" he exclaimed in accented Franca. "Why do you come here?"

Adara kept Sierlas in her sheath. Lemas had a point – they were not here to slay the magus, but to beg his help. "Frasios of clan Berandion sent me to consult with you, O mighty Melandurin," she replied in Merudur. The magus blinked. A human woman, immune to all his spells, speaking the language of his people (if with an abominable accent) and addressing him by name? It made no sense.

"I know no such person," Melandurin told the intruder coldly. Adara dipped her head respectfully.

"Perhaps not," she said, "but your fame is widespread. In Prizlion you have become something of a legend. My companions and I knew not where else to turn, so we have come seeking your aid."

Stranger and stranger! But she had made no move to attack him – an attack he would have been hard-pressed to halt, since his magic was apparently useless against her. The necromancer relaxed his posture, and beckoned her closer. "Come, I will not harm you," he said. "Let us go into my abode, so that we can sit and discuss your reasons for disturbing my solitude."

# Chapter 19

Adara let Melandurin lead her through the door into the tower. He was an inch or two shorter than Lemas, and darker than most merudur she'd met. His skin had a definite blue cast, the hair on his head a medium blue-gray, with indigo eyes that looked almost black in the dim light within the entryway. He seemed neither old nor young, his ageless features having a cold cast to them. Well, she was hardly expecting a reclusive necromancer to be a jolly fellow, was she?

They did not climb the steps to the tower, but instead went back down a stone-carved corridor to an area that appeared to be the magus' living room. For having apparently been carved into the side of a mountain it was surprisingly comfortable, with carpets and wall hangings and some furniture not dissimilar to what Lemas' family had in their home near Prizlion. A cool blue-white light was provided by crystals glowing in wall-mounted sconces – far brighter than phorium. Adara wondered what they might be. Something sorcerous?

Melandurin beckoned to her to take a seat. She half expected him to wave his staff and cause refreshments to appear; but instead he stepped to an alcove and returned with a tray on which were two metal goblets and a pitcher of what turned out to be spring water.

After seating himself, the necromancer studied his visitor. Definitely, she was human – though she was nearly as tall and slim as a woman of the merudur. But she looked so young! His desire for solitude was fighting a losing battle with his curiosity, as she thanked him and took a long drink of water. That had been an arduous climb!

Seeing that her host was looking at her expectantly, after swallowing her glass of water Adara spoke. "My name is Adara Willoughby," she said. "I'm a citizen of Tanar, and an amateur archaeologist. My companion, Lemas of clan Azarion, and I have been searching for the lost Sword of Myralis, and Frasios – who is an archivist at the Royal Historical Archive in Prizlion – told us that there was no information for us there. He suggested that you might be able to call up the spirit of Myralis, so that we could ask *her* what became of the fabled sword"

The necromancer sat back in his chair, his hands steepled on his lap, and peered at her. "I wonder how well-informed this Frasios is," he said after a moment's thought. "I seriously doubt there would be no information about Prizal at all in the royal archives. And perhaps he forgot to mention to you that I have been using my arts to exclude all comers from my island for the past several hundred years? Were it not for this curious power you have of warding off magic, you would be dead now."

A terrible suspicion came over Adara. Frasios was Diurla's former consort. But surely, she would not seek to send her stepson and his companion to their deaths? Melandurin went on, "That curious creature I saw flying toward my fastness, was that affiliated with you?" Adara nodded.

"Malika, my semigryph companion," she acknowledged. "We intended no harm, only wanted to learn where this place was so that we could consult you."

"We?" the magus asked. "Is this Malika a sentient being, a demon of some sort?"

"Just an intelligent animal," Adara explained. "Her kind live in the east-central part of Tanar, and when I was there last year I rescued her after she had broken her wing." She considered how much information to impart, not wanting to give too much away, but decided there'd be no way to hide it. "I have a mental bond with her, and can see through her eyes."

Melandurin raised an eyebrow. Still another remarkable aspect of this rather appealing young woman! He had felt no desire for the company of his fellows in centuries, but her presence stirred something within him. She was not even of the udur, a mere short-lived human, but she had an indefinable aura. Intelligence, determination, confidence – and behind that cool exterior, passion like a great cat sleeping, ready to blaze into action. He wondered what she was like in bed, and stifled the thought immediately as he felt a throb from his long-disused groin region. Could it be she truly was a magus, and was casting some kind of lust spell on him? He was profoundly annoyed that it seemed to be working.

"I would like to have my companions join us, merun Melandurin, if you will give your word that they will not be harmed," Adara said. "I promise you, we will not take up much of your time." Take all you want, a little voice whispered in the back of the necromancer's mind, and he brushed it aside.

"I will not harm you or your friends," he promised. "But I expect you to be gone as soon as our business is concluded."

Adara nodded, and stared off into space for a moment. Then she reported, "They are on their way from the cove where we came in, and should be here by midday or a little after." In her mind's eye, she saw that Lemas had gotten the message and was climbing the path even as Malika took to the air again. She soared in circles above him as if urging him on. A pity he, too, could not fly!

They had more of the cool, refreshing spring water and some hard flatbread with cheese while they waited, and Adara related the tale of their search for Prizal. "You have something belonging to the queen, then?" he asked sharply, and she drew forth the signet ring. They had left the gaudy sword, and the bulk of their belongings, back at Lemas' family's house.

"That is good," he said. "Without such a thing, it would be nearly impossible to contact the spirit of Myralis, let alone draw her to speak with us." Adara was fascinated. The religion of Tanar held that the souls of the dead most commonly went to an otherworldly afterlife – a sort of mirror world wherein those who had been good in life would be rewarded while those with sins on their souls – thievery, murder, and so forth – would find their circumstances reduced. A schismatic sect within the church claimed that this afterlife was also a proving ground, and that by one's actions there one would be reborn into the world again – at a station determined by those actions.

"Do the spirits linger nearby, then, that you can contact them?" Adara asked.

"Some roam our own plane of existence, unable or unwilling to move beyond it though their bodies have died," Melandurin explained. "Others have gone on to the spiritual plane, wherein reside gods and djinni and the other beings of spirit. But for those of us with the gift, it is not hard to communicate with them there. Whether they are willing to answer, is another story."

Huh. Just like the elementals, Adara realized. Did the eastern sorcerers have the same problem getting djinni to do their bidding, if they were not coerced as Fatiha Baba had been? "You are not able to force the dead to respond to you?" she asked. The necromancer looked uncomfortable.

"There are… ways," he admitted reluctantly. "But they are difficult and distasteful. It is far better to obtain the cooperation of the dead, than to attempt to command them." Adara nodded thoughtfully. It occurred to her that an unwilling spirit might well give completely false information, unless the compulsion required it to speak the truth.

They had begun delving into Adara's earlier adventures, Melandurin seemingly unwilling to discuss his reasons for living alone here on the island – or any details of how he obtained the necessities of life like food and clothing. Elves might live for millennia, but their clothing would wear out just like anyone else's. Abruptly she got a sending from Malika: We're here, where are you?

She rose to her feet. "My companions have arrived," she said. Her host stood as well, and they went back out through the now-closed front door to find Lemas standing beside the semigryph. Melandurin heaved an internal sigh. He suspected this stunning specimen of young merudur manhood knew *exactly* how Adara was in bed; but it wasn't likely *he* was going to find out.

Instead, after a brief introduction, he focused his attention on the semigryph. Malika's fur rose and she hissed at his approach, until Adara adjured silently, make nice! Reluctantly, she stalked forward and rubbed against the magus' legs through the ankle-length robe he wore. He instinctively reached down and scratched her behind the ears, winning her tentative approval.

"Remarkable!" Melandurin said. "Will she come inside?"

"She's been known to do so," Adara allowed. "But I think she'd be more comfortable waiting for us out here. She's hungry, and she'd like to do some hunting."

"Very well," the magus replied. "I'm sure we could all use something to eat. Please come in."

To the astonishment of his uninvited guests, the necromancer shortly brought in a tray of sandwiches and fresh fruit. The bread seemed recently baked, the fruit chilled. Adara had been rebuffed earlier when she'd asked him questions about his living arrangements, and she merely eyed him questioningly, an eyebrow cocked.

Put out, Melandurin grumbled, "Suffice it to say, I am not the original owner of this humble abode. I inherited the place from its former owner, a merudur magus who had studied in the lands to the east. I have but to request food from a magical chest in the kitchen, and it appears. And no, I have no idea how it works."

Adara smiled at him, an expression that lit up her pretty face and gave the necromancer another pang of regret. Maybe having a consort wouldn't be such a bad thing, he thought. Not a human, obviously – she would have to be a woman of the merudur. But what woman would be willing to live here in such isolation? And he simply could not tolerate prolonged contact with his fellow men, especially given the ill favor with which his life's work was regarded in merudur society. For centuries, his only companions had been the spirits he conjured. Some of them were congenial enough – but you couldn't have sex with them.

"It's a shame you don't have the making of such a device," Adara said. "Imagine how wonderful it would be when traveling or adventuring, to have whatever delicacy you desired without any effort!" He nodded.

"It has certainly made living here on this desolate rock far more pleasant," he admitted.

When they had finished their luncheon Melandurin rose to his feet. "Come, we will go to my tower now and see whether Queen Myralis is receiving callers." Adara exchanged a glance with Lemas, excitement simmering inside both of them. Against all expectations, they were going to get what they came for. Would it work?

The tower, built out from the cliffside while the rest of Melandurin's dwelling was carved into it, rose some one hundred feet above the level of the courtyard from which Adara had entered. Glassless windows pierced its walls to the south, west, and north at intervals, but the east side was part of the rocky peak itself.

Contrary to Adara's expectations the thirty-foot-wide tower did not contain the eight or so floors you might expect to find in a structure of such height. There was one intermediate floor at around twenty feet from where the spiral staircase had begun, a circular room with a fifteen-foot ceiling that appeared to be used as a lumber room. It was full of cast-off furniture, dusty pieces of magical apparatus, and the like.

That floor's ceiling was *not* the floor of the space above it, however. They climbed the staircase up and up – occasional windows on the outside, blank stone walls opposite – until they reached the tower's top room. It reminded Adara only vaguely of the room at the top of the Bloodspire where, riding a gyrfalcon, she had observed the Mancer King at his scrying bowl a little less than a year ago.

The floor was stone, and around the circumference of the room various items of presumed magical apparatus were positioned. The domed ceiling rose nearly fifty feet above their heads, and here there were no windows. Both Adara and Lemas found themselves drawing in a breath, looking around them with apprehension. There was not precisely a sense of evil, but they definitely felt they were in the presence of the arcane.

Their host smiled, more of a grimace. What a strain we must have put on him, Adara thought sympathetically. Yet he had risen to their invasion with surprisingly good grace. "I will need the ring, Miss Willoughby," he said, holding out a hand. She deposited Queen Myralis' signet into his palm.

Adara and Lemas hung back near the wall in a narrow section free from furnishings, as Melandurin prepared to call Myralis. They were both fascinated, not that either of them had any ambitions to become necromancers. Adara took a moment to let her mind reach out for Malika, making sure she was all right. The semigryph had found an area of the plain below the island's central peak where fat ground squirrels made their homes (and how in all the hells had such creatures gotten here to this island, more than a hundred miles from the nearest major land mass?), and was enjoying herself immensely trying to catch them.

The center of the room was given over to a circle some six feet in diameter, delineated by a line of what Adara took to be brass set into the stone. Around that circle, a line of similarly-inlaid runes flowed. They were not the runes of the ancient merudur, she realized. How long had this place been here?

In the exact center of the circle was a three-foot pillar of white stone, different from that with which the tower had been built. On it rested, or perhaps was carved from the same piece of stone, a shallow bowl. Melandurin gently set Queen Myralis' ring into the bowl, then performed a series of mystical passes over it while intoning something that sounded like no language Adara had ever heard before. Mumbo-jumbo to impress the audience, or ancient mysteries witnessed now for the first time in ages?

Next, to the surprise of the onlookers, the necromancer removed a small dagger from a sheath at his belt. The blade was matte gray, black runes engraved in it. He extended his left arm over the bowl and cut a thin line along it just above the wrist. As blood welled and began to drip into the bowl with the ring, he began chanting in a low voice – more of those syllables that held no meaning for either Lemas or Adara.

Was it life to call the dead, Adara wondered? She had been told by Nanny Selden that blood freshly drawn from the body was as alive as the body itself – for a short time. Abruptly Melandurin's chanting broke into recognizable Merudur, as he intoned "Queen Myralis, champion of the merudur, I beseech you. Return to the world of the living for a while, that we may hear your words of wisdom."

There was a flash of blue light centered on the bowl, and a spectral figure rose from it like smoke – towering above them thirty feet. No wonder the ceiling of the chamber was so high! The space to spread out must be a lure for the self-important spirits of the dead. "What would you have of me, Melandurin?" the spirit demanded in tones echoing like wind chimes and dripping with hauteur.

# Chapter 20

It was Queen Myralis, all right. Both Lemas and Adara clearly recognized the face of the woman whose corpse they'd encountered in the tomb near Meruzal. For this spectral command performance, however, she had chosen to appear in what they guessed must be the armor she'd been wearing when she died. It wasn't half as fancy-looking, and at her enlarged size the dings and dents in it were plain to see.

Adara nudged Lemas forward. "You talk to her," she murmured. She couldn't imagine the ancient merudur queen would be pleased to be addressed by one of the upstart humans who'd eventually driven her race from the continent. He rose to the task. Lemas' level of confidence had soared since embarking on this quest and obtaining Adara as a lover – if not truly as a consort, like he'd been telling people.

"My queen," he said in a ringing voice, stepping forward to gaze up at the blue-glowing form. A slight smile ringed the spectral features as she beheld him. "I am Lemas of clan Azarion," he went on, "and it is on my behalf that Melandurin has called you."

"Very well, speak!" the queen ordered. It was clear that in her time, she had commanded the utmost respect. But Adara sensed that Lemas had somehow made a good initial impression. He was, of course, the most fantastically attractive merudur male she had ever laid eyes on. But that was just her. The pureblood merudur girls he'd grown up around had spurned him.

"It has been nine thousand years, more or less, since Your Majesty was lost to us in the final battle against the pinudur," Lemas said. He was speaking firmly and clearly, with no hesitation, and Adara felt a little thrill of pride. The boy had come a long way in the last few weeks.

"So long," Myralis replied, with a hint of sadness. She remained silent for a moment, reaching out with her psychic senses Adara assumed. "My people are now mostly confined to Elyrion, but they prosper," the elven queen went on. "What is your concern, Lemas of the Azarion?"

"I am a smith, Your Majesty," Lemas went on. "From a long line of Azarion smiths. And among us, the tale of Prizal – crafted by your consort Rohiran – is legendary. But none know what became of that mighty sword. I have learned that it was not interred with you, but have found no record of where it might lie. I would restore it to the merudur people, as a national historical treasure."

Wow, perfect, Adara exulted. He had totally *not* mentioned the fact that a mere human was the instigator of the quest, or that he and she had jointly desecrated Myralis' tomb and killed off all her bespelled guardians. We'll make an adventurer of you yet, young smith!

"Ah, Prizal," the spirit of Myralis said in echoing tones that suggested infinite weariness. "I must explain to you the nature of that blade." Adara, Lemas, and Melandurin as well were agog, waiting for her to speak more. "Rohiran crafted Prizal for me when first I was chosen queen," Myralis said. "He was the love of my life, and I his. And the sword was a wonder. For not only did it grant me dominion over my enemies in battle, it gave me the power to lead others, and the wisdom I needed to do it in a way that would benefit all. It was the sword Prizal, not my own native abilities, that made me a great queen of Silaine."

Seeing that her audience was spellbound, the enormous specter went on. "I defeated every enemy on the field of battle at Gadsen. None could stand before me, while I wielded Prizal. But Rohiran's magical blade could not ward me from treachery. Even as the pinudur threw down their arms and cried out for mercy, I was struck in the back by an arrow tipped in poison."

"From someone on your own side?" Lemas asked, aghast.

"So I am convinced," the queen replied. "Though I knew not who fired the shot. I died, and my consciousness became… dispersed, for a time. I lingered, learning that none knew who had killed me. I watched as Rohiran, crazed with grief, condemned those of my guard who had lived while I died to an eternity of loneliness and suffering. It was not their fault."

Adara nodded sadly. In retrospect, it seemed that she and Lemas had done those poor Guardians a favor. "And the sword?" Lemas prompted, caught up now in his role of interrogator of the dead. "It went to my daughter Susalna, of course," Myralis responded. "When Rohiran created the sword, he gave it a sort of consciousness. It was not truly a being, but it had loyalty – loyalty to the line of Rohiran and Myralis, and especially to those members of that line who had been bonded with it. Susalna was but a small child when the sword was created, and we brought her to bond with it immediately so it might know her, and extend its gifts to her. She was still a very young woman at the time of my death."

It was a little bit like the Darkshield, Adara realized – passed down from mother to daughter. "And what became of Susalna?" Lemas asked.

In tones of satisfaction, Myralis replied "She was chosen queen of Silaine at the special moot occasioned by my death. And she was re-elected ten more times, ruling our people for more than a thousand years. Such was the power of Prizal, to ensure a ruler for the merudur both popular and wise."

"You remained in the physical plane then, Majesty?" Lemas asked. "Watching over your descendants?"

"Indeed I did," the once-queen replied. "It was far more interesting, even though I lacked the power to affect the physical world, than roaming the spirit world would have been. I saw my line through triumphs and disasters, as the millennia passed."

"And Prizal? What befell Prizal?" This was the central question they had come here to ask, and all three of them hung on the answer. It seemed that Queen Myralis was more than willing to tell them everything, possibly having spent the last several thousand years waiting for a chance to speak.

"It remained with my line," the specter replied, waving slightly in the air above them. "Though not in the way I might have hoped. Susalna's great-granddaughter – ah, I cannot recall her name – took as consort a human man she had chanced to fall in love with. There is something about humans, I think, the brightness of their brief flame, that calls to us whose lives are so long. In any case, she bore a son – a son she loved so dearly that she bonded him with Prizal when he was not a month out of the womb."

Gods preserve us, Adara thought, realizing where this was going. Myralis continued: "The boy swiftly grew to manhood, and the queen realized her mistake. She had sacrificed her fertility to produce a child who would be dead of old age in less than a century, and given up her line's claim to the throne of Silaine. For she bore no other children, and Prizal could be bonded with no other line."

"The sword had become irrelevant?" Lemas asked, shocked.

"Oh no," the specter replied. "The human son of that once-queen of Silaine, when he had become a man, took Prizal as his birthright and left to become a king among the humans. For its powers granted him the ability to win men to his cause, to guide wisely, and to defeat all who sought to oppose him. I believe it was he, this mayfly descendant of mine, who founded the kingdom that would become Tanar."

Gods! Adara thought, shocked. She was a little sketchy on her ancient history, but it was said that the modern kingdom had arisen from a small but powerful enclave centered around the current location of Carlienne. All because of Prizal? But then what had become of it? The ancient elven sword was clearly *not* part of the current ruling family's ancestral treasures. And they had only been the ruling family for less than a thousand years, in any case.

Adara and Lemas were reeling at the spirit's revelations, Melandurin merely bemused. Isolated as he had been for nearly half his life, he had lost his sense of connection with the history of his world. Queen Myralis went on, "Prizal continued to provide the line of that human descendant of mine with charisma, wisdom, and invincibility in battle for many generations. The kingdom of Tanar grew by conquest and negotiation, and the merudur nation of Silaine fell. My people, my true people, were exiled to Elyrion while the humans – including my own human descendants – spread across the continent. I was torn, for I must admit that humans can be very entertaining." She glanced at Adara for the first time. Adara felt a little like a bug under a magnifying glass.

"And then what happened?" Lemas asked. "How was the sword lost?"

"Through a very human failing," the spectral queen replied. "Some five hundred years after my first human descendant took the sword, his most recent heir had carried it to a place near the coast of the Surden Sea on a campaign to defeat rebels who were resisting the annexation of what was then the kingdom of Merseine to the kingdom of Tanar. He was a young king and a vigorous one, newly come to the throne and not yet wed. When he fell to a sudden fever, his men knew only that the sword was an heirloom of his house. And since he was the last of his line, as they judged such things, they decided to inter the sword beside him to do him honor. They had no idea of Prizal's powers."

"He was not truly the last of the line, then?" Lemas asked, having caught the specter's implication. It was apparently not possible for a ghost to snort. But Myralis did bark a laugh, of sorts. "Among humans? Of course not! There were hundreds of them by then. Humans breed like rabbits, had you not noticed? But many of them were 'born on the wrong side of the blanket' as the humans put it, they with their marriage rituals. The crown went to a fourth cousin, or some such. Ridiculous degrees of relationship, these humans have. But the sword remained hidden away, interred with its last wielder."

"You know this, Majesty?" Lemas asked, with a hint of excitement in his voice.

"I have followed that sword since my death," the specter replied simply. "I was bonded with it, and one in every generation of my descendants was also bonded with it, until at last it was laid to rest with Gregan. It lies there still, beside his moldering body, in a cave along the shore above the Surden Sea."

This was wonderful, better than they could have hoped! Of course, the southern coast of Eorla was more than a thousand miles wide, all of it abutting the Surden Sea. But they finally had a location, and right from the queen's mouth – so to speak.

Lemas' beautiful face was shining in excitement, in the blue-white light of the mysterious crystal lamps that robbed him of some of his warm human coloring. "Can you give us landmarks, Majesty?" he asked. "We would seek the sword and return it to the merudur people."

"Oh assuredly," the spirit of Queen Myralis replied. "You, Lemas, are of my line through your mother Julia – the first of that human line to return to pureblood merudur. I choose you to recover

Prizal, and bond with the blade. You will lead the merudur people back to supremacy, and drive the humans from Eorla."

# Chapter 21

When Adara and Lemas were ready to leave, they were surprised at Melandurin's request: "Take me back with you to Prizlion."

"But you have been happy here for centuries," Adara protested. "Are you sure?" The necromancer dropped his gaze, made uncomfortable by the need to explain himself.

"Your arrival, and that of your companions, has brought to my attention an area in which my life is lacking," he admitted. "I need to… expand my horizons, before I return to my life of solitude." He needs to get laid, both Adara and Lemas thought without speaking. They were young, and the answer was obvious to them. It had been far less obvious to Melandurin, but he had eventually arrived at the correct conclusion.

"Very well," Adara said. She was wearing Fatiha Baba, had been wearing it since their arrival on Barrow Island. "Lemas and I will be retrieving our animals and belongings and then taking ship south," she told him. "I can leave the portal open, so that you – and anyone you might want to bring with you – can return through it. But it would then remain open."

"You can close it," the necromancer replied immediately. "I can easily return home by other means." Adara nodded. She had Fatiha Baba open a portal from the courtyard outside Melandurin's fortress home to an uninhabited spot less than a mile from the outskirts of Prizlion. Since realizing the necklace's potential she never went anywhere without storing mental pictures of her surroundings.

They parted ways with Melandurin as they walked into town, heading for the stables where the horses and Debardo were stabled. The animals had been residing there for less than four full days. "Thanks and good luck," Adara told the necromancer. She stood on tiptoe and kissed him on the cheek, which caused him to flush almost purple. Then she and Lemas went on their way.

Lemas squeezed her to him, and heaved a sigh. "Do you realize what chaos you sow, my love?" he asked philosophically.

"Whatever do you mean?" Adara replied innocently. He squeezed her again, this time seizing her right butt cheek through her tight leather trousers.

"Every heterosexual male you meet wants to throw you down and fuck your brains out," he asserted.

Adara felt, surprisingly, a little offended. "It's not my fault," she replied defensively. "I'm not even most guys' idea of an ideal woman. Why would you say that?" Lemas turned and enfolded her in a tight embrace.

"I'm probably just projecting," he admitted. "It's *me* who wants to fuck your brains out. Could we do it right now?"

Grinning but still a little ticked off, Adara stepped out of his embrace and slugged Lemas lightly on the arm. "Later, you!" she declared. "We still have to collect the animals and check in with your family, then figure out how we're getting to the south coast." He stood chastened. After a while they walked on.

"I can't see how we can get there any faster than taking ship," he said.

"We could portal to Meruzal and take ship from there," Adara suggested.

"Yes, but there isn't a tenth as many ships leaving from there as from Prizlion," Lemas pointed out. She had to concur.

Returning to Niemas' household led, inevitably, to the issue with Diurla. "I'm sure she put Frasios up to sending us to Barrow Island in hopes it would get us killed," Adara asserted. "I didn't mention the Darkshield to her or to anyone else in Elyrion, and without it we'd have been dead."

"You're probably right," Lemas responded with a sigh. "Diurla is a conniving bitch, and she's been hoping I'd conveniently drop dead ever since Dresan was born. But I love him, and my father loves him. He's welcome to Father's estate, and I'm not going to provoke a confrontation with his mother."

What could Adara do but go along? Still, she obtained a wicked satisfaction from seeing the expression on Diurla's face when she and Lemas, with their animal entourage, turned up at the house on the coast to reclaim their belongings. They gathered those belongings, had another night of passion in Lemas' childhood bed, and in the morning said goodbye to Niemas and Dresan before going back to Prizlion to book passage for Riveil.

Merudur mariners sailed far and wide, to ports all over the world. The *Strihalian*, a three-masted vessel as graceful and streamlined as the gulls that were her namesake, took only a day and two nights to arrive in Meruzal. After a few hours there spent loading and unloading, she was off on the evening tide – hugging the Westwater coast as she made for Riveil.

The journey to Tanar's westernmost Surden Sea port took another four days and nights, and the travelers had a long, slow, and pleasant break from the frantic pace they'd been engaged in since their quest had begun. Adara and Lemas made love in their comfortable cabin several times a day, and spent the rest of their time visiting with the animals, strolling the decks, or just sitting on deck and conversing – between themselves, or with some of the other passengers. *Strihalian* was as much a passenger ship as a trader, and her accommodations were quite comfortable.

The ship docked in Riveil in mid-morning on the fifth day, and two of the other passengers disembarked as well. The rest would be going with the ship further on its long voyage, east along the Surden Sea coast and then south for a tour of the ports in northern Frigan as it returned west toward home. Adara, leading the frisking Zarhya down the ramp, wondered at such a lifestyle.

The anti-seasickness potion had worked well again, making the voyage a pleasure; but being cooped up on even a ship the size of the *Strihalian* for days at a time was not something she would have sought except for the need to be carried to her destination much faster than she could have gone overland. Now that she was here in Riveil, storing up mental impressions, Fatiha Baba could open a gateway here whenever she wanted to visit again. The thought filled her with satisfaction.

"I suppose we had better put up for a night in an inn here," Adara mused aloud. "We're going to need supplies before we set off across country." There was a good east-west highway in southern Cornmarch, well-strewn with coaching inns and farming villages. But it ran miles inland from the coast, and they needed to travel right down by the water so they could watch for the landmarks Queen

Myralis had described for them. The specter had confirmed that she had looked upon the site of Prizal's resting place in modern times, and those landmarks still existed. It had been around fifteen hundred years since the childless King Gregan had died and been entombed with his sword.

"Mmm, maybe we can get a hot bath before we set off into the wilderness," Lemas suggested. Adara had introduced him to the sorts of fun a couple might have in the process of getting clean, and he'd become a much bigger fan of hot baths as a result. If the water was deep enough, it was like making love in midair.

Adara eyed her lover sidewise and grinned. She had to admit that the boy had talent. For a novice herself, in a very short while she had been able to teach him many ways to send her soaring to ecstasy. Him having a strong flexible body and that monster cock helped, of course. But his tenderness and his passion were the traits that made him such a wonderful lover. She sighed internally. Once they had the sword and Lemas had been initiated as the heir of Myralis, he would have his own destiny to fulfill. And there would be no further role for her in it. They were going to have to part, and soon – but not yet!

They took a room for the night at the Seaview Hotel, an upscale modern-style four-story establishment that did indeed offer a view of the Sunder Sea half a mile to the south. After the horses were stabled they set off on foot, guiding Debardo by his lead rein, and went shopping in the nearby mercantile district. They bought a tent, an extra-large bedroll for Lemas, and some cooking gear along with non-perishable food supplies for their journey. Malika, as usual, had gone right up into the stable's hayloft for a nap.

They stabled the mule with the horses after returning to the hotel, then ate a late lunch in the dining room. The place reminded Adara of the new hotel in Willoughby where she'd stayed with Stellan last year, and she felt a little pang as she thought of that lost love. Just as with Lemas, she had steeled herself going in for the possibility that they would not last as a couple. Stellan was so withdrawn, so secretive. And never once had he told her, "I love you." Nor had she said it to him.

It was the same with her and Lemas. Though the love was there, shining in his eyes, he had not forgotten her very sensible warning before their first time together. She'd been momentarily infuriated with him for telling his family she was his consort, until he'd convinced her it had been just a ruse to be sure they were allowed to share a bed. She wondered, sometimes, what was going on in that fine mind of his.

"What shall we do for the rest of the afternoon?" Adara asked, as she was finishing her meal. It had been fish (of course), but prepared in a delicious way with herbs, spices, and mushrooms. As Cornmarch was the source of much of Tanar's food, so their cuisine was famous across the continent for its flavors and variety.

"It's a lovely afternoon," Lemas said with a happy smile. "Why don't we change into some cooler clothing and go for a stroll along the waterfront? This looks like an interesting port." They made a striking couple, the tall slender young woman in a flowing cotton dress and her still-taller, powerfully-built elf escort. Many a head turned to gaze at them as they sauntered past, hands clasped.

Riveil was one of the largest and most bustling ports in Tanar, getting the Surden Sea trade as well as ships from across the Sunset Sea and the Westwater to the north. Curious-looking vessels from ports in Frigan, the Sultanate of Khouresh, and even from far-off Westaria (inhabited mostly by slender, rather short humans with straight black hair and skins the color of toast, so Adara had read) could be found among the more familiar ships of Tanar and Elyrion.

Seabirds called, the breeze brought them the scents of tar and fish and salt, and they came across a colorful street market where vendors offered clothing, jewelry, produce from the farms in the area, and spices from around the Surden Sea. A street performer dazzled passersby with juggling and sleight of hand, and Adara found a stall offering many familiar herbs. She was able to restock her supply of potion ingredients, including the crucial motherwort.

She'd become quite accustomed to adding the powdered herb to her food or beverages daily, preventing any man's seed from taking root in her womb. But wouldn't it be nice, she mused, if there were a magic ring or something like that to prevent pregnancy? It would be a disaster for her to get with child, especially Lemas' child. What if it turned out to be an elf?

Though if her "hidden elven blood" theory was correct, it was unlikely that Adara carried any. Her line had come from far to the east of the merudur's haunts. If there was any elven blood in her, it was more likely that of the pinudur – who long ago had ruled over most of what was now Nordstan, and contended with the aurudur for domination of the area now called Northmarch as well as with the merudur in the west.

She squeezed Lemas' hand, thinking sadly of the fate that must soon part them. "Hey," he said, gesturing ahead, "What's that?" Among the open stalls and blankets spread out on the stones of the broad plaza beside the docks, a purple-and-green tent had been pitched.

"Looks like a fortune teller's hut," Adara told him. "There are a lot of Gitanos in Cornmarch. They roam around in caravans from town to town, mending pots and telling fortunes for the most part. A lot of nonsense, really, and some claim they're thieves who will take anything that's not nailed down. But if you'd like to, we can go see. I'll pay."

He grinned down at her. "Sure, why not?" he said cheerfully. "In Elyrion there are magi and wise women who will cast the auguries, and some of them can be pretty accurate – especially if you give their predictions several centuries to come true. I'd be interested to see how they do it here."

The tent was eight feet high at the center and maybe fifteen feet across. Lemas had to duck to come in through the flap, though. Inside, by the light of a pair of oil lamps mounted on wrought iron stands, they beheld a colorfully-dressed old woman seated behind a small round table. She looked to be in her seventies at least, silver hair peeking out from beneath a kerchief, her hands gnarled with arthritis. As the visitors came toward the table the old one looked up, and Adara could see that she was blind – the once-black eyes gone milky blue. A little shiver ran through her.

"You have come seeking the wisdom of Madame Rosa," she pronounced in a surprisingly firm voice. Adara smiled. Ah yes, the all-seeing eye of the mystic crone. Though the fact that this woman's eyes would be of no use to her at all *did* add a touch of the mystical to the experience.

"My companion would learn of his future," Adara told the fortuneteller. "Approach then, and give me your hand," Madame Rosa commanded – in the general direction of where Lemas stood, a slight smile on his lips.

He stepped up to the table and extended his powerful yet graceful, long-fingered right hand. You could tell a lot about somebody just by touching their hand, Adara realized – age, occupation, past injuries... She was unprepared when the Gitana suddenly gasped, seizing Lemas hand palm-up in both of hers and running her fingers over the lines on his palms. Other than some differences in facial features and build, and the fact of their slow development and long lifespans, elves were little different from humans. Palmistry should certainly be just as effective with them. But Adara didn't think it was the creases in Lemas' palm that were giving this woman her information.

"Your Majesty!" she breathed. "King of the Merudur, scion of the line of Myralis! I and all my descendants for more than a thousand years will be dust, ere your reign shall end!" Lemas pulled back a little, startled and frightened. He had told Adara he had no intention of fulfilling the specter's expectations.

Lemas knew, if the long-dead queen did not, that humans now outnumbered all races of the udur by a factor of at least ten to one in Eorla, and likely by still more elsewhere in the world. There was to be no Prizal-led merudur invasion, no driving of the humans from the continent. The current king, Tersin, had tried that on a tiny scale, and look where *that* had led. True, he had not had the backing of the fabled magic sword – but there was only so much a sword could do.

The old woman seemed to have recovered from her vision, or whatever it was. Continuing to hold Lemas hand, though he half wanted to wrench it from her grasp, she went on more calmly. "You are linked with a woman... a *human* woman!" she said in surprise. After a moment's thought she said "This one here." Looking at Adara with her blind eyes, she commanded "Come here. Give me your hand."

Reluctantly, Adara reached out and let the crone take her hand. Lemas, released, took a step backward and watched half in horror as the Gitana read his lover's palm. "You are linked to his destiny," the old woman said, "but you are not to be a part of it. You have your own destiny to fulfill, still many years from now." Right, no doubt I'll meet a tall dark stranger, or perhaps marry a prince, Adara thought. She had been startled by Rosa's prediction for Lemas, but this sounded pretty generic. He was an elf, she was a human woman, of *course* she was not going to be part of his destiny.

The old fortuneteller had closed her sightless eyes, as if that somehow helped her concentrate on her inner visions. Suddenly her face took on a look of alarm, and she hissed, "No! Oh, evil! Beware the red djinn!" The eerie eyes popped open again, boring into Adara's as if they could see into her soul. "Love will give you joy, and sadness. But beware hate! Do not hold hatred in your heart, or it will bring you to destruction!"

Adara had had enough of this. Drawing her hand back, she plucked a handful of coins from the purse at her belt and flung them onto the tabletop. Then, taking Lemas by the hand, she said "Thank you, Madame Rosa, for your predictions. We must be going." She stalked out of the tent, pale in the spring sunshine.

Trying to make light of the unsettling experience, Adara led Lemas over to a street stand selling crepes. As they watched, the man dipped batter onto his hot, round griddle and moments later rolled the crispy pancake around some fruit preserves. As they walked away sharing their treat, she said lightly "So, you're going to rule the merudur for a thousand years! That sounds like quite a career…"

Lemas sighed. The old woman's words had filled him with uneasiness. How could she have known such details, when she could not see him and he had not even spoken a word in her hearing? "I'd really rather be a smith, I think," he said.

"Can't you be both?" Adara asked. "Surely, the merudur are by and large a group of mature, sensible people. Being king couldn't really be a full-time job."

He grinned at her. "You haven't seen my 'mature, sensible people' squabbling at a clan moot," he said. "But yeah, compared with human societies we're pretty stable. It helps to have long memories. Likely I could continue my studies in smithing. But I would have to move to Prizlion. That's sort of a job requirement. Anyhow, even if I showed up tomorrow waving Prizal, it's going to be another thirty-odd years before the next moot. And I'm just a kid. The clan chieftains are all three or four times as old as me, at least, and they generally elect one of their own. I think we're getting worked up over nothing."

Adara sighed. She hoped he was right. She cared deeply for Lemas, even if she wasn't prepared to admit that she was in love with him. Just because she wanted to spend every day in his company and every night rolling in his arms, didn't mean she was in love. And as for that nonsense about a "red djinn" – well, if she did make it to the Khanate to learn about eastern magic, that might be good advice. She'd just as soon avoid *all* djinns, no matter the color. Though now she thought about it, Fatiha Baba was all right.

Lost in her swirling thoughts, Adara suddenly realized that they had left the street market behind and could walk no further to the east. "What do you say we go back to the hotel and see about that bath?" she suggested.

# Chapter 22

In the morning Adara and Lemas made love again, knowing this would likely be their last chance to do so in a large and comfortable bed for some time to come. She had camped out a great deal over the past year on various quests and adventures, but Lemas had never done so – raised in a comfortable home, taken in at his grandfather's smithy, then sleeping with her in a series of inn beds and ship's cabins. She hoped he was going to take to it all right.

Loaded up with their supplies and with Malika riding atop Debardo's packs, they rode in single file through the streets and boulevards of Riveil until they had found their way out of town. The coast immediately to the east was rocky, with low cliffs and many small streams cutting paths southward. There was usually a cove with a little sandy beach where each of these met the Surden Sea, and they found that the narrow trail they followed frequently went down onto these beaches. It was slow going.

It was a pity that the spirit had lacked the ability to pinpoint exactly where along the coast the old king's tomb lay. She had been able to manifest her awareness there due to the presence of both the sword and the body of her descendant, just as she was able to do so in range of any of her other descendants – or, more fully, through the spells Melandurin had used to call her to his tower. In other circumstances, she was just a formless, invisible wraith. Adara supposed it was a good thing Myralis' spirit lacked the power to affect the physical world – she was likely to be a little ticked off when Lemas declined to follow her instructions regarding the future of the sword, and that of the merudur nation.

They knew that a small river, big enough for rowboats to navigate, came down to the sea beside a tall bluff with trees growing on it. And about halfway down that bluff, facing the sea, was a natural cave. A narrow rock ledge had formed a trail down from atop the bluff to the cave, and once wildcats had denned there. But when fever had struck down the young king hundreds of miles from his castle in Carlienne, as he and his army were encamped enroute to lay siege to the last stronghold of the king of Merseine, they had laid him to rest in that cave and walled it up with stones taken from the shore.

The plan had probably been to return for the king's body, and take it back to Carlienne to lie in the royal tomb with his ancestors – after the army had laid waste to Merseine's capital and added its land to the growing kingdom of Tanar. But the same fever that had killed the king had swept like wildfire through the ranks, and before the army had reached their goal they were so decimated and weakened by disease that they had been picked off and utterly destroyed by their enemies. Neither King Gregan nor the army that had accompanied him ever returned to Carlienne, and it had taken centuries more before Tanar's expansionist ambitions had risen again.

Adara had found the tale in a book on modern Eorlan history Niemas had on hand, though of course it had not mentioned anything about Prizal. It made her feel a little odd to realize that though the events in the book had occurred more than a thousand years ago, they were considered very modern by the author of the book – a merudur scholar specializing in human studies, who had been alive at the time King Gregan had ruled in Tanar.

There were dozens of small rivers flowing down out of the hills south of the Grandeon to the Surden Sea, and the one beside which Gregan was laid to rest might be any of them between Riveil and Seaspire – the modern small port city built on the site of the former capital of Merseine. After the Tanar conquest, when the former southern kingdom had become part of Cornmarch, the capital had been moved to Grenier on the banks of the Grandeon.

During the course of the day they passed two small rivers – neither of them running beside a bluff. They had to ford any streams they came to, as all of the bridges were several miles north on the main road. The sky along the coast was gray, and there was a stiff breeze blowing; but the weather wasn't that bad for traveling in. Malika slept most of the day, curled up in a little hollow between the packs on Debardo's back. But when they stopped to rest and eat, she would immediately fly off to the shore. The semigryph seemed to have developed quite a taste for ocean fish, a delicacy her wild cousins would never have tasted.

Finally late afternoon was coming on, and Adara realized that it was time to start looking for a place to camp for the night. They had passed a few fishing villages on their journey, but none of them offered any amenities. On the other hand, one could camp nearly anywhere one wanted to along this sparsely-populated stretch of coastline. There were no farm fields to trespass on, no dogs to run off trespassers.

Adara spotted a line of trees on the horizon, which must mean another of those small rivers. She immediately cast her eyes to the right, hoping to see a bluff overlooking the sea. No such luck. But the river should provide them with water for cooking and washing, and the trees with a modicum of shelter. She put her heels into Zarhya's flanks, and urged her into a canter. With the many obstacles they'd had to negotiate, their pace had been sedate and the tough Khoureshi mare could have kept going for hours yet. She was glad of the change of pace.

Lemas, who had Debardo in tow behind Sadiq, maintained the fast trot they'd been moving at. He guessed Adara was eager to reach a camping spot, and they'd catch up shortly. The trees were scrubby, windblown evergreens – cypress, perhaps, with a few small willows growing down along the banks. The bottom of the small stream was silt, the water no more than three feet deep even here not a hundred paces from its mouth.

After the mare had bent her head to take a drink Adara pushed Zarhya across, just able to keep her feet dry. The vegetation was somewhat thicker on the eastern bank, and after climbing up out of the riverbed she turned north to where some larger trees were growing. Here, in a little grove with a bare spot in its center – this should be a good enough campsite. Adara dismounted, and took her pack down off the rear of the saddle before removing the saddle.

A minute later the rest of her party arrived. "Have you ever camped out before, Lemas?" Adara asked. Somehow, with everything else they'd had to discuss, this question hadn't come up. "When I was a kid, in the mountains west of Prizlion," he said with a grin, fond memories playing in his head. "Just tell me what to do, and I'll do it."

She grinned back. Her huge elven lover was as cheerful as Ferdyn, but considerably more pliable. "Let's get the packs and saddles off the animals," she suggested. "They'll need to be rubbed down and given some grain. Then, if you can go down to the beach and fetch us some driftwood for a fire, I'll get the tent set up." Lemas threw her a slight salute, and set to work dealing with the horses and mule. He might not be an outdoorsman, but he'd been caring for horses since early childhood.

Hours later, replete from a meal of camp stew and stale bread, they huddled side by side watching the flames. Smith-strong Lemas had outdone himself on wood detail, bringing not only double armloads of wood for the fire but a six-foot, foot-in-diameter driftwood log for them to use as a bench in their campsite.

He threw his arm around his lover. The Gitana's words had struck home, and he was growing ever more aware of how precious their time together had become. Under the best of circumstances they would have had a few decades; but he knew they'd be lucky to get a few more weeks. Tipping Adara's chin, he kissed her deeply.

"I wish the weather were nicer," Lemas said with a sigh. "I've been fantasizing about making love in the great outdoors with you ever since we got together." The onshore breeze that had been blowing all day had turned cold, and fog was coming up from the shore. At least there was no rain to put out their campfire.

Adara kissed him again. "A spring meadow full of sunshine and wildflowers *would* be nice," she mused. "But we could still do it right here in front of the fire…" Lemas eyed her curiously, his imagination working overtime. "I'll be right back," she said, rising to her feet and going toward the tent. It was a small thing, with a height at the roof peak of around three feet, four feet wide and eight long. She crawled inside, and when she emerged a couple of minutes later Lemas saw to his surprise that she'd apparently changed out of the leather pants she'd been riding in and was now wearing an ankle-length full skirt.

He raised an eyebrow in question as she returned, smiling mysteriously, to sit beside him again. "Now, where were we?" she purred, and took him in her arms. They remained seated side by side on the log for a few minutes, kissing and stroking and squeezing, until both of them were panting with desire. Lemas eyed the sandy, rocky, soil of the campsite, and then looked a question at Adara. She was at work on the lacings of his trousers, and in a moment had brought forth his towering cock from its concealment. The cold air was like a shock, cooling the heated member but somehow inflaming it still more.

Adara bent and worked it over with her mouth and hands, squeezing rhythmically and sucking until it glowed, glistening in the firelight. "Um…" Lemas got out between gasps. For answer, Adara lifted up the hem of her skirt and guided his hand inside. The minx was wearing no underdrawers! And her slit was soaking wet…

Spreading the full skirt out like a picnic blanket, Adara stepped over Lemas legs so she stood astride him, face to face. Then she carefully lowered herself down, engulfing him. Aah! She let the skirt fall, shielding their bare parts from the chill night air, and began moving up and down on him even as she locked her mouth on his. Oh, yes! Lemas seized her buttocks through the cloth of the skirt, helping her to bounce on him as the sensations, and the unfamiliar setting, carried him along like an avalanche.

In the morning, they were up and breaking camp almost as soon as the sky became light. The fog had gotten thick overnight, but by the time they were ready to mount up again it was beginning to tatter in the stiff breeze, retreating to lie like a gray wall a few hundred yards off shore. Malika had prowled and fed during the night, and was once again sleeping between Debardo's packs as they resumed their slow progress east along the Surden Sea coast.

They had fresh ocean fish for supper that night, compliments of Malika with a little gentle urging from Adara. The semigryph was becoming such an effective hunter that she was capable of catching far more than she could eat; and with her instincts making the activity pleasurable she was happy to oblige.

They had had several more hours in which to travel today by comparison with yesterday, and had crossed eight streams ranging from yard-wide rivulets to a small river that had required them to jig four miles to the north – half the distance to the main road – to find a spot where they could ford it. But they had not seen the landmarks they hoped for.

Three hours into the third day of travel they at last spotted something that looked promising – another small river cut through the coastal plain, fifty feet wide this close to its mouth. On this side the banks had eroded to a gentle rocky slope, falling gradually to the beach where half a dozen shallow channels cut through the sand and gravel to spill into the sea.

And above that point to the east, a rocky bluff rose nearly a hundred feet above the strand. Small scrub trees grew atop it, and seabirds wheeled above it as the surf crashed against the sand at its base. There was a moraine of gravel leading up from the beach, suggesting eons of erosion of the cliff face.

Adara and Lemas exchanged a glance, grinning. This could be it! The bluff, which was close to a hundred feet wide, was sheer along the river's eastern bank but sloped down to the east and north until it blended with the coastal plain. After picking their way down to the strand and splashing across the river on the beach, the travelers continued east on the sand and fine gravel until they found a place a hundred yards further along, where they could climb back up. Then they faced west again, and mounted the bluff's eastern slope to reach the top.

To complete Adara's joy, the sun was beginning to come out – the depressing gray overcast that had persisted almost constantly since they had taken ship from Prizlion breaking up into puffy gray-white clouds. The top of the bluff commanded a great view out to sea, and she could see the sails of distant vessels plying the waters to their south.

Her smile as radiant as the sunshine, Adara dismounted and gave Zarhya a pat. She let the reins hang down, and the mare began looking around with interest at the vegetation coating the top of the bluff. Back some distance from the southern edge, it was almost like a little forest up here.

His heart singing with excitement, Lemas climbed down and stood beside his lover looking out over the sea. Malika had peeled off when they had gotten onto the beach earlier, but now she came flying back – a wriggling silvery fish about a foot long in her jaws. You can have it, Adara sent. She wouldn't mind some fish for dinner, but she hadn't been planning to cook for lunch – and maybe by suppertime they would be back in Prizlion!

# Chapter 23

At Adara's behest, once she had devoured her fish and performed her all-important ablutions, Malika took to the air again and soared in circles above the bluff so that Adara could see whether they had truly arrived at the right place. Sloping down from the top of the bluff on its west side, where it fell sheer to the river, she spotted a faint line that might have been a deer trail – if there were any deer here. They hadn't spotted any during their journey, but there had been a few wild goats.

Let's take a look at the side facing the sea, Adara requested, and Malika obediently wheeled to face that side. Yes, inside a dark recess there was an area of the crumbling bluff that was built up of many stones, mortared together into a crude wall! "This has to be it," she told her companion excitedly. "Come on, let's get the packs off of Debardo and dig out the tools."

Based on Myralis' description of Gregan's final resting place, they had acquired a mining pick and a wrecking hammer along with other supplies on their shopping trip in Riveil. The horses were freed of their accouterments and left to forage on the bluff top. It was unlikely they'd be going anywhere.

Adara and Lemas took a moment to refresh themselves, munching on trail bread and drinking water from their skins before picking up the tools and making their way between the sparsely-growing evergreens to the western edge of the bluff. Fifteen hundred years ago the trail leading down to the cave in the cliff face had probably been easily broad enough for a man; but in the intervening years it was likely nothing bigger than foxes or rabbits had used it. It was perilously narrow, eroded away in places, and treacherous with loose gravel.

"I don't like the looks of that," Adara said, and Lemas nodded in agreement.

"Let me cut us a couple of walking sticks before we start down," he suggested, even as she had another thought. While he used the razor-sharp irilium dagger he bore to cut a couple of appropriate staffs from the trees growing on the bluff top, she rummaged through the packs and came up with a long coil of thin, strong rope.

Adara walked the western edge of the bluff to a point around halfway between the start of the trail and the place where it turned the corner to go around to the southward face – where the cave was. Then she found a sturdy, low-growing cypress branch and knotted one end of the rope securely around it. Paying the line out as she went, she began walking between the cliff edge and the trees until she struck the trailhead again. Lemas was just coming back with a couple of sticks.

They were not very straight, but they were sturdy and reasonably stiff. He saw her standing there with what remained of the coil of rope in her hands, the rest of it trailing on the ground along the cliff edge to their south. "Great idea!" he said cheerfully, handing her the shorter of the two sticks. Adara looped the rope around his waist, knotting it, and then tied the tail end of it around her own. There was around eight feet between them. Should she slip and fall, it was likely Lemas would keep his feet and be able to haul her back up. If it were he that fell, they would probably both go over the side – but at least they could use the rope to climb back up.

Better if *neither* of us falls, Adara thought, as she gripped the pick in her left hand and the walking staff in her right and followed Lemas down the barely-visible trail. She had put on her mountaineering boots, the ones she'd worn for the expedition into the Ratskells last summer; but all he had were the boots he'd been riding in. They had heavy leather soles with little grip to them.

It appeared as if the trail had actually been chipped into the cliff face, perhaps enlarged by King Gregan's army in order to facilitate the project of entombing their dead monarch in a safe location. But more than a millennium of sea storms and rainfall had covered its surface in rough gravel that slipped and shifted under their feet as they made their way along. Without the sticks to help them maintain their footing, they'd have been dangling from the rope above the river in no time.

Around thirty feet along they came to a spot where the rock supporting the trail had crumbled away completely, leaving a gap of around eight feet where there was nothing but nearly-sheer cliff. Lemas looked up the cliff, down which their rope dangled, and then down at the raging waters of the small river flowing below. "Adara, I think you'd better cling to my back," he said as he began pulling the slack out of the dangling rope.

She followed his thought, and closed up the gap between them. "How am I going to hang onto you with my hands full?" she asked. Lemas managed to slip the heavy hammer, with its three-foot handle, through his belt. Neither of them had brought their swords, though both had daggers. Adara put her pick through her own belt, where it gouged her hip painfully. Then after she had hopped up onto Lemas' broad back like a toddler playing pick-a-back with an indulgent older sibling, he slipped their walking sticks down between their bodies. It was horribly uncomfortable.

Taking up their weight on the rope carefully, afraid it might break, Lemas lifted them both up the cliffside above the trail and began walking against the sheer wall crabwise, moving across the gap. Fortunately they were not yet directly below the tree to which the rope was secured, and that made it easier. Less than a full minute later, they were standing on the trail again.

"Maridem defend us, I hope there are no more of those gaps," Adara said. "I think I'm going to be black and blue as it is." Lemas enfolded her in a tender embrace and kissed her forehead.

"At least we won't have to walk back," he pointed out, and raised a grin.

There were no more gaps. They turned the corner, and in another ten paces found themselves at the entrance to the cave. The trail widened out here to a ledge around four feet deep – enough space for those ancient masons to do their work. Adara wondered that they had happened to have mortar along with them on that southern military campaign. Perhaps they had intended to build some permanent fortifications after they'd gotten where they were going?

The mortar, though inset some distance from the surrounding cliff face, had suffered greatly from its exposure to the sea air. As had been the case with the mortar holding the irilium bars in place at the entrance to the kobold's air shaft near Feingeld, the lime had been leached from it over the centuries and it was crumbling. The cave opening was scarcely any taller than Lemas himself, but he had room to swing that hammer – with all the power his long arms and blacksmith's muscles could bring to the task.

Adara soon realized she could have skipped taking the pick along. Compared to her companion, she might have been a child playing with twigs. They both wore goggles, protecting their eyes from flying debris, and she backed off a few paces to stay out of his way. The cave opening was no more than eight feet wide, and there was not all that much room for two to work even if she'd been his equal.

Fifteen sweaty minutes later Lemas had cleared the majority of the stones and mortar from an area near the right side of the opening – four feet wide and nearly seven high. He leaned the hammer head down against the remaining portion of the wall, and drew a forearm across his brow. He was grinning.

So was Adara. She felt a profound sense of excitement, anticipation… and dread. Were they about to do something they both would regret? She pulled their Siiri lamps out of her pack and handed one to Lemas. "After you, O king of the merudur," she said with a bow. He grimaced at her, but held the lantern in front of him and stepped through the opening.

Adara was right behind him, eyes wide as she beheld the cave's interior by the warm glow of their lamps. Gods, there he was! The cave was small, quickly tapering back from its maximum seven-foot height at the entrance to nothing but a crack in the rock some twelve feet further in. The corpse of Gregan, once king of Tanar, lay on the floor on the left side of the space, still sheltered by what remained of the masonry wall.

The centuries had not been kind to him. He was clad in steel armor that had once been enameled with the crest of Tanar's royal house, but it had mostly rusted away. What they could see of the face beneath the rusted helm was skeletal, no trace of flesh remaining. In the damp climate of the seacoast, it would probably have rotted completely away in only a few decades. The body was lying on a pile of organic-looking dust, which on closer inspection Adara decided had probably been a bier of cypress boughs. They would have improved the smell in the small chamber, for a while. But they hadn't held up as well as their occupant. Half buried in that dust, at the king's side, a glint of unrusted metal could be seen.

Lemas' eyes grew wide in the dim light. He felt almost as if he could hear a voice calling his name – whispering, beckoning. He spotted the gleam of silvery metal and knew it for irilium. Prizal! Helpless to stop himself, he seized the sword hilt – and stood transfixed, as a flood of images were forced into his brain. He saw Queen Myralis as she had been in life, wielding Prizal in defense of the realm. Her daughter Susalna, who had ruled in wisdom for a thousand years, visiting the sword from time to time and drawing from it the qualities of wisdom and leadership – but never using it in battle.

In quick succession other leaders of the line of Rohiran and Myralis flashed before his mind's eye, and he knew each of them for who they were, and what deeds they had done while bonded with the sword. A few more elves, two men and a woman, and then dozens of human men after that nameless human ancestor, with his hidden elven blood, had carried it off with him to become a ruler among the humans.

To Adara's eyes, watching Lemas' reaction, the sword seemed nothing more than a particularly nice and rather antique-looking iridium sword quite similar in appearance to Sierlas, the hilt decorated with jewels and the blade etched with runes. To Lemas it blazed with a blue-white light, calling wordlessly to him with its unique magic. It had come home, was once again in the hands of an elven descendant of Myralis' line – and it was ecstatic. The experience was more powerful than any orgasm he had ever had, and he'd had some doozies since Adara had come into his life.

Adara stepped near and put a hand on Lemas' arm, peering up into his face. "Lemas, are you all right?" she asked anxiously. He hadn't spoken a word for two minutes, his eyes fixed on some distant point at the back of the cave. The parade of ancestors had run its course, and he was now able to wrest back his consciousness from the magic sword. He still held it gripped in his right hand, though.

Lemas looked into Adara's eyes, a curious expression on his face. "She... Queen Myralis... was right," he breathed. Then louder, "I am the first fully elven descendant of Rohiran and Myralis in thousands of years! Your theory was right, Adara! My father's pure elven blood mixed with the elven blood hidden within my human mother. She may have imparted some human characteristics to me, or they might just be the characteristics of one of my elven ancestors. Not all the merudur look alike, after all. But I'm not a 'half-blood,' as my people have been calling me since I was born. I am fully merudur, and any children I have with a woman of the merudur will be pureblooded elves as well."

Adara stifled a pang. What more could she hope for, than having Lemas part with her on friendly terms and go off to be with a woman of his own kind, one who could give him a child who would outlive him? Why, then, did it hurt so much? Love could be so damn stupid. She thought back on Ferdyn, whom she'd loved wholeheartedly for a time; and Stellan, whom she'd loved in spite of herself. When was she ever going to learn? She sighed slightly, and squeezed Lemas' arm where her hand still rested on it.

"So the sword has bonded with you?" Adara guessed aloud, and Lemas nodded.

"It showed me every ancestor who's ever been bonded with it, starting with Myralis," he explained.

"And is it begging you to take up arms and drive humans from Eorla?" she asked with a touch of asperity.

"Gods, no!" Lemas exclaimed. "It doesn't actually talk, you know. It's more like what you've described about your bond with Malika than what you get interacting with Fatiha Baba. More like mental pictures, emotions… It's really, really happy to be in the hands of an elven descendant of Myralis, though. I suppose it was lonely all those centuries, shut up in this tomb."

Adara was fascinated in spite of her feelings of unhappiness and anxiety. "I suppose you're actually only the sixth elf to bond with the blade," she pointed out. "It's been in human hands far longer. But it was made by an elven smith so that the merudur might have wise, just rule. I guess it's only natural for it to be glad you found it."

Fatiha Baba opened a portal at the rear of the cave, just beyond King Gregan's body, back up to the top of the bluff where their animals waited. Adara and Lemas began gathering their things. The scabbard Rohiran had made for Prizal had apparently been made of something more perishable than irilium, and the blade had been bare when they found it. Lemas added his steel elven longsword to the pile of items atop Debardo's back, and put Prizal into its sheath. The blades were of similar size and shape, and it fit well enough. Though he was already formulating plans to craft a fitting scabbard for the legendary sword.

Adara noticed that since bonding with Prizal Lemas had seemed very loath to let the blade get more than a foot from his hand. Was it like a new mother bonding with her baby? And how was that going to work with his stated intention to turn Prizal over to the Royal Historical Archive in Prizlion?

Finally all was in readiness. Lunchtime had come and gone, but neither of them felt hungry. Adara looked to her lover. Was there an aura around him, a sense that he was someone she should look to for guidance? She realized that the Sword of Myralis had provided many generations of human kings with just those qualities, so clearly the spell worked as well on humans as it did on the merudur. It had profoundly shaped the history of her own nation, at least the early parts of it.

"Well," she said finally, bowing to the inevitable. "Where are we going?"

"Home," Lemas answered without hesitation. "Father's house. The beach below, where we came in from Meruzal the first time, will do nicely." No hesitation, and Adara immediately felt like obeying his... orders? Suggestion? It gave her very mixed feelings.

# Chapter 24

Fatiha Baba needed only a reference to the location where they'd first arrived in Elyrion a couple of weeks before, and the view of that fog-shrouded beach appeared before them – in a square easily big enough to pass both of them and their mounts.

Soon the portal had been closed again, and the small party climbed the trail to the top of the cliffs and made their way the short distance to the house of Niemas and his family. Dresan was out front, working in the gardens, when they arrived. Very few of the merudur were employed as servants, though most of them would spent some time in life performing menial tasks. These were seen as necessary to living, and nothing to be ashamed of.

"Lemas! Adara! You're back!" he cried excitedly. His big indigo eyes spotted the shining jeweled hilt of the longsword riding above his older brother's left shoulder, and went wide. "Is that…?" Lemas grinned, and bent to enfold the boy in a bear hug.

"That it is," he said in tones of satisfaction. "Is Father here?"

The boy nodded. "He's in his studio, as usual." It had been mid-afternoon atop the bluff in southern Cornmarch where they'd stood half an hour before, but here it was just mid-morning. "Do you want help with the horses?" Dresan asked, and Adara happily assented. They got the animals unloaded, rubbed down, and stabled with some oats to chew on – though today had been an easy one for them after the past few. Then they all went into the house.

They had noticed that one of the family's horses was missing from its stall, and learned that Diurla was not here. Lacking any real calling like art or music, she often became bored hanging around the house while Niemas was immersed in his painting. She was in the capital visiting with friends – and stirring up mischief, Adara would be willing to bet – several days per week.

They went inside the house and found Niemas at his easel, working on a somewhat smaller painting than the one that had stood there on their first visit. To Adara's astonishment, she realized that it was a picture of her and Lemas standing outside this very house. Had her arrival triggered nostalgic feelings about Lemas' mother, she wondered?

"Father, we got it!" Lemas said, drawing the sword carefully after coming through the doorway. Ceilings in merudur dwellings were tall, but their doorways were usually no more than seven or eight feet high. Niemas turned with a look of astonishment and delight, and gazed at the gleaming blade. Despite having spent more than a millennium lying in a damp cave buried in rotten vegetation, it had needed only the swipe of a cloth to make it look new again.

The painter set down his palette, his eyes wide, as he gazed on the fabled Sword of Myralis. It was truly exquisite, not only a supreme example of the smith's art – let alone its magical properties – but a *work* of art. One he, as one of the foremost artists of his generation, could readily appreciate. Then he looked into the eyes of his elder son, joy shining there. They were of a height, and so similar in appearance except for Lemas' warmer coloring and more muscular build, that they looked like twins.

Again Adara was struck by how odd it was associating with people who might well be able to throw parties at which eight or nine generations of the same family – most generations represented by only a single individual – might be in attendance. And except for the very youngest and oldest of them, they'd all look about the same age. She didn't know how old Niemas was, but surely he must be close to five hundred at least. Yet there was no trace of aging to be seen on his beautiful features.

"Your face has changed, my son," Niemas said softly.

"The shade of Queen Myralis did not lie," Lemas replied. "I am truly her heir, just as she said. Mother bore the elven blood, and perhaps that is what drew you to her. And I am as fully merudur as you, though half my heritage passed hidden through dozens of human generations. In any case, Prizal has bonded with me, chosen me for its bearer."

Now Niemas' look of pride and affection turned to one of concern. "It means to have you lead our people to ruin, trying to drive humankind from the continent of Eorla?" he asked in horror. Adara and Lemas had told him all that had passed during their visit with Melandurin. Lemas put a hand on his father's shoulder and squeezed it affectionately, a slight smile on his lips as he shook his head gently.

"That was Myralis' idea," he said. "She has watched her line through many human generations and surely ought to know better, yet she is out of touch with the realities of the modern world. Prizal's gift to me is the charisma to draw others to my leadership, the ability to defeat any foe in combat… and wisdom, Father. Wisdom tells me it would be insanity for the merudur to go to war – with the humans, or anyone else. We are secure on our island, and free to roam the world in peaceful trade. Preserving that situation is in the best interests of our people."

Niemas smiled in relief and embraced his son. He was an artist, a pacifist who cared nothing for the "glory" of war. Yet King Tersin had been able to fire his countrymen into attacking the might of Tanar in an effort to wrest control of Elvany back from the usurping humans – a costly and ultimately pointless effort. With usually no more than one child per family, elves were ill-suited for war. Merudur women had lost their sons, their daughters; and would be unlikely to have any to replace them.

Lemas stepped over to the table on which his father mixed his paints, and carefully set Prizal down upon it. Adara was surprised he'd been willing to let it get that far from his body; but perhaps the imprinting was starting to wear off. From what she'd gathered about Myralis' daughter Queen Susalna, the woman had kept the sword tucked away and rarely brought it out – for the thousand years of her reign.

"What now, son?" Niemas asked.

"We need to have a discussion with Muralos of clan Azarion," Lemas replied without hesitation. Again Adara was surprised at his confidence, his take-charge attitude. He was not the same sweet, hesitant young elven smith she had taken as lover only a handful of weeks before. Prizal had literally turned him into a leader of men during the few seconds when he had first grasped its hilt. Oh, what had she done?

Dresan, thrilled with the exciting turn of events, was more than happy to volunteer as runner. He would saddle his horse and go to the Azarion Clan House in Prizlion, there to request Clan Chieftain Muralos' presence for supper at the home of Niemas, one of the most renowned members of clan Azarion. He was also instructed to pick up some groceries while he was in town, as it was unlikely his mother would look with favor on unexpectedly being required to feed the most important member of her consort's clan. Adara gave him a shopping list.

"Do all the clan chieftains headquarter in Prizlion?" Adara asked, after Dresan had run off and the three of them were gathered over lunch in the villa's dining room.

"Not all," Niemas said. "Elyrion is a large island, though far smaller than the continent of course. With it being forbidden to take a consort from within one's own clan, and with children joining the clan of whichever parent shares their gender, the clans have become quite dispersed. But there are pockets, here and there on the island, where clans live side-by-side and tend to breed only with each other. Most of us in the Prizlion area disapprove of this, thinking it tantamount to incest – as over the generations most members of the two clans are related to each other by blood."

"But those clan chieftains stay in their enclaves, and don't reside in Prizlion?" Adara guessed.

"Exactly," Niemas went on. "The clan system is ancient, and in the earliest times the clans were nothing but large extended families, ruling over traditional territories. In modern times, they have become more like clubs or fraternal orders… and perhaps a bit like political parties. But ones you are born into, not ones you choose. In any case, most of the more forward-thinking clans have members spread all over the place, and Clan Houses in Prizlion where the chieftains reside – ready to advise the monarch, or even perhaps overthrow him or her if the situation requires it."

"And clan Azarion is one of the more forward-thinking clans…" Lemas chuckled. "One of the oldest, and one of the most modern," he went on. "Actually the area around Prizlion, before the fall of Silaine, was our clan's 'traditional territory.' It was natural for the Azarions to be one of the first to establish a Clan House when the new capital was founded."

Fascinating, Adara thought. Her emotions were clouded by her unreasoning love for Lemas and the sure knowledge, held from day one, that it was never going to work. But she thought that the merudur, as one of the more accessible races of the udur, could easily constitute a lifetime's study for any human scholar. Maybe someday she would return to them, and learn more. They had so many advantages over humans, just as humans had many advantages over them. And the two species were inexorably linked, the elven heritage capable of remaining hidden in human bloodlines for hundreds, thousands, of years.

Late afternoon arrived, followed shortly by Dresan. He'd brought with him saddlebags loaded with meat, vegetables, and other foodstuffs. Also, a confirmation that Clan Chieftain Muralos had accepted the dinner invitation. Adara immediately set to work planning her meal – she had not cooked for more than a couple of people in ages – while Dresan, Lemas, and even Niemas set to work making sure the house was clean and in order. The merudur were naturally a tidy people, but Niemas' creative endeavors tended to distract him from housework. And Dresan was an adolescent.

Diurla, the lady of the house, arrived an hour later to find the house spotless, her kitchen taken over by that human trollop, and her despised stepson in residence and now in possession of the powerful ancient artifact she had confidently believed lost forever. She was not pleased. That displeasure escalated when she learned they were hosting the Azarion clan chieftain for the evening.

During the decades in which Diurla had been Niemas' consort, Muralos had only twice graced their table with his presence. It was the artist's fame, as well as his striking beauty, that had drawn her to him after all; and hobnobbing with the elite of clan Azarion was to be expected. But she had not cared much for the man, and still less for his cold, calculating consort Erlina.

The woman had a way of looking right through you, her piercing pale blue eyes seeing to your core and finding you wanting. Not that she was impolite, or anything – but there was no deflecting that adamantine intellect with the kinds of subterfuge Diurla was accustomed to use. They had worked so well on Niemas, had they not? And for a brief time in their relationship, she had truly loved him. Else, Dresan's conception would not have been possible.

Diurla retreated to her private bedchamber, where she slept most often these days in preference to sharing her bed with Niemas, and sulked. Where had it all gone wrong? Lemas, with Prizal in his hands? And he now confirmed as the heir of the legendary Queen Myralis – through the line of his inferior human mother? It was almost too much to bear. She busied herself selecting the most elegant gown, applying makeup and jewelry until she was a vision no heterosexual merudur male could resist. She might have suffered setbacks, but she was still the most beautiful woman clan Cabrilion had produced in several generations.

Muralos and his consort arrived by carriage after dark, as Adara was putting the finishing touches on the meal she'd slaved over for the past several hours. The carriage had been driven by one of Muralos' subordinates at the Clan House, who hoped to rise in the clan hierarchy and was happy to make himself useful. He'd already eaten, and would sit patiently waiting for the clan chieftain to come out so he could be driven back to Prizlion.

Adara had decided to go with a dish that was popular in Rivermarch, tender chunks of beef simmered in red wine with mushrooms and small white onions. It was served over noodles she had rolled out herself, alongside a large bowl of mixed spring greens tossed with red wine, vinegar, oil, and herbs. Fresh bread crusted with garlic and cheese completed the simple menu. She prayed she wasn't too far off base with what she assumed would be unusual fare for Elyrion. The fact that all the ingredients had been readily available suggested that merudur cuisine couldn't be that different from what was served on the continent.

As Adara toiled in the kitchen, assisted by Lemas (who kept distracting her by pinching her butt, most annoying), Niemas suavely entertained his clan chieftain and the chieftain's consort in the sitting room – accompanied by Dresan and Diurla. It wasn't until she was putting the food on the dining table that Adara got a look at Diurla post-primp, and she was struck speechless. Gods, the woman was utterly exquisite!

How could a soul so petty and conniving lurk beneath an exterior that looked as if it had been carved by angels? Adara was reminded sharply of Chtorias, the evil sorcerer of the Siiri, who had been so beautiful she'd had half a mind to lie down and spread her legs for him instead of lopping off his head. It was fortunate that good sense had prevailed.

The food was well-received, and Muralos and his consort were quite courteous to the human upstart who'd prepared the meal. Adara felt relieved, but the powerful sense that she didn't belong here was only growing as the evening wore on. Lemas, sensing her discomfort, reached under the tabletop and squeezed her hand. They were still operating under the pretense that she was his consort.

The conversation at the table was light, cheerful – it was a social occasion, not the first move in a political game that could affect the rulership of Elyrion for centuries. Adara noticed that Diurla seemed remarkably brittle, trading barbs with the slender and graceful Erlina.

The clan chieftain's domestic partner couldn't hold a candle to Diurla for sheer physical beauty, but she seemed to have her beat by a mile when it came to brains – nor did she appear to hold Lemas' stepmother in any great regard. Yet you'd be hard put to name anything she said as an insult or even an indirect put-down. Adara was in awe of the woman's abilities, and wished she could emulate her. Though what she really wanted to do with Diurla was throw her up against a wall and slap her around a little. The cow had tried to get her and Lemas killed!

For dessert Adara had baked a couple of apple pies, familiar and delicious Rivermarch treats Nanny Selden had taught her to make. They were served with clotted cream, and exclamations of delight were heard around the table. Then, finally, they all adjourned to the sitting room and the real business of the evening could get underway. Adara supposed that it only made sense for people with all the time in the world to take a while getting to a point.

Lemas carried in the Sword of Myralis from where it had been lying on the table in Niemas' studio since he'd set it down several hours earlier. There were gasps from Muralos and Erlina, but Diurla had already seen the blade and pretended not to be impressed. Inside, she was seething. Why in all the hells couldn't that necromancer simply have killed his uninvited visitors, as Frasios had assured her would be the case?

"Prizal has bonded to you?" Muralos asked, scarcely believing he held the fabled object in his hands. As he was not of Myralis' line, it had no more effect on him than would any other blade – or the fork with which he'd eaten his pie.

"It has confirmed me as the first fully merudur heir of Myralis and her consort Rohiran in many millennia," Lemas said.

"Fully merudur?" the Clan Chieftain had to ask. "It's my understanding your mother was human?" Lemas smiled, and Adara could almost see that smile winning over his audience. She was already in love with him, so it didn't affect her as much.

"The spirit of Myralis confirmed a theory my consort Adara had proposed," he went on smoothly. "The elven blood does not mix with the blood of humans, but is dominated by it when human and merudur interbreed. Yet the human-seeming offspring of these alliances, like my two long-dead human siblings, carry within them their elven heritage – hidden away, ready to come forth in future generations."

Muralos and Erlina seemed stunned. Since hardly anyone they knew had ever spent much time in the company of humans, they knew nothing of the phenomenon of changelings. Lemas went on, "It is likely that among the human population of western Eorla there are thousands who carry merudur blood. And when two of them mate, or when one of these half-elven humans mates with an elf, there is a chance that the resulting offspring will get the elven blood from both sides – and be a full-blooded elf. As I am."

The Clan Chieftain digested this for a few moments, then burst out, "We must call a moot! A clan moot!" While the moots at which merudur monarchs were chosen occurred at intervals of a hundred years, clan moots could be called at any time the current chieftain felt it was necessary for the clan to gather and make important decisions affecting its members. It was not obligatory for every clan member to attend, but any who did not were throwing away any chance at political influence.

"That will take weeks, will it not?" Lemas asked. While the majority of clan Azarion's members lived in the area around Prizlion, some of them were spread far and wide. Clan members must be notified, and given time in which to attend. Else the pretense of granting individual members political power was nothing but a sham.

"Of course," Muralos replied.

"I don't want to wait weeks, followed by more weeks," the young clansman replied. "I think it is time to call a general moot. A special moot, to decide whether King Tersin will remain in office." Muralos and his consort once again looked stunned. But Adara could see them falling into agreement with what Lemas proposed. He'd mentioned that there'd been much political unrest regarding Tersin's failed military campaign. Had Prizal's "wisdom" function informed him it was time to put an end to it? This was scary.

"Yes," Muralos said, after considering the question for less than a minute. "It is time. With Prizal returned to us, the hour is at hand. You are an untried young man barely into adulthood, who has inadvisedly taken a human woman as consort, and was thought to be of questionable mixed blood. Yet from what you've told me, breeding with humans might only be a way to help us catch up with them – a chance for each merudur man to father more children. If there were a way for us to identify these human women with hidden merudur blood, each man might be able to have two or more purely merudur children!" He seemed to be getting more excited about the breeding issue than was consistent with decorum, but it *was* a revolutionary idea.

Both Diurla and Erlina were looking appalled. Having merudur women become second choice to human women on the basis of their inability to produce more than one child in their long lives was *not* something any merudur woman was likely to regard with favor. Adara sympathized. Besides, this notion of human women as broodmares to pop out a few merudur kids and then die of old age was repellent. The man who fathered your children should be your life partner, she thought – not some stud elf looking to expand the number of his progeny.

Muralos had not finished his thought. "I will discuss this with the other clan chieftains in Prizlion," he promised. "Despite your youth, Lemas, I think you might be the candidate for king around whom the forces opposed to Tersin can rally. With Prizal in your hands, we may be able to rid ourselves of the warmonger without having to wait another forty years to do it."

# Chapter 25

Adara lay with Lemas in his childhood bed, her mind in turmoil. "But *why*, Lemas?" she demanded, resting her head on his shoulder after he had made love to her for nearly an hour. Despite her concerns, the power of his sexual energy had driven her into a frenzy. Only now, in the afterglow, was her mind functioning again.

"The conflict over Tersin and his ill-considered war is bad for Elyrion," Lemas explained patiently. "While the majority of the clans, or at least of the chieftains, are willing to let him slide until the next scheduled Royal Moot, the festering resentment is tearing our nation apart. We need to have a special moot, and we need to change the law so we don't have to wait for an entire century to deal with monarchs who have violated the sacred trust and betrayed the merudur people."

Since realizing that he was one hundred percent merudur, it seemed to Adara, Lemas had begun identifying with them much more strongly. Or was it just the power of the sword? "So, if the moot is called and they decide they want to dump King Tersin, what happens next?" Adara asked.

"The assembled clan chieftains will vote on a new monarch," Lemas explained. "There will be a full day of nominations, with each chief allowed to nominate a candidate. Then on successive days, votes will be taken. The advocates for the candidates, or the candidates themselves, are allowed to address the moot before the voting begins on the second day. After that, votes are taken again and again until one candidate has a majority."

"Good gods, that sounds like it could take forever," Adara said.

"In practice, it's usually less than a week," Lemas replied confidently. He seemed to have been transformed from an astonishingly cute but gormless blacksmith into a political maven, overnight. "The current monarch, in this case King Tersin, would remain in office until a new one was chosen. And there's no law against nominating the incumbent, for that matter," Lemas went on. Adara rolled her eyes. Maybe her initial impression, that the merudur's system of choosing their leader was superior to the primogeniture system of Tanar, was mistaken.

"And if they elect you?" Adara murmured. He squeezed her tightly to him.

"Then I will take up the mantle of the king of the merudur," he said softly. She rolled over and buried her face in his smooth, nearly hairless chest. Hot, salty droplets moistened the skin, though she said nothing.

Within days, they learned that the special moot had been called. Muralos was evidently a persuasive man, and seemingly the time had come. Though Lemas' magically-enhanced charisma had not been directly involved, merely his description of the young paragon who had been chosen by Prizal as the heir of Myralis was enough to convince most with whom he spoke – after decades of inconclusive arguments - that a moot should be convened.

Adara had no idea what effect these events had had on King Tersin. Since he was likely to become one of the few kings in merudur history to be booted out after serving less than a full term, she assumed he would be less than thrilled to hear the news. A human king would have been sending out his agents to cut the right throats, she supposed; but for a king who ruled at the will of the clans, it seemed there was nothing he could do but sit there and wait to be deposed.

On Lemas, the prospect of the forthcoming moot seemed to have no effect at all. He acted as if nothing could be further from his mind than the possibility he might be elected king of the merudur people in the next couple of weeks. His desire to make love with Adara day and night was undiminished, and it was he who suggested they get Fatiha Baba to open a portal so they could go and visit in Pine Hill, and with Adara's family in Willoughby. She didn't know what to make of it all.

Nanny Selden was well, her young protégé Ellie Forrest prospering and learning the herbalist's trade. Adara's old beau Jason Miller and his bride, Nelly, had a beautiful baby boy. Seeing what a proud father the former horndog had become gave Adara a bit of a pang. But she had no real hankering for the life most girls in her home village had chosen.

As they opened a portal for Underhill, Lemas asked her "That Jason fellow, he was your boyfriend once?" It must be that wisdom thing again, she supposed, feeling annoyance.

"We used to flirt when we were kids," Adara acknowledged. Baring her soul, she admitted "I thought I might jump his bones and take him on as questing partner last year, before I discovered he and Nelly had gotten married."

Lemas put his arm around her and squeezed her to him, a gesture of affection that almost rent Adara's heart. His charisma was such that every scrap of attention he paid her made her love him more. It was driving her insane. "I'm hard put to imagine any young man in his right mind would have passed up a chance to be with you," he said sincerely. "He must have presumed you were dead."

Adara felt a surge of warmth at his words, along with a surge of love that sent her deeper into bleak despair. She could not bear to part with Lemas, and she *must leave him* as soon as possible! Damn that sword to all the hells ever imagined by the mind of man!

They spent a week visiting with the Underhills and Willoughbys, and to Adara's great shame she and Lemas visited the swimming hole near the farm and made love on its banks. The water was far too cold this early in the year; and the experience ruined the memory of her first time with Stellan, in that same location. That night in Adara's upstairs bedroom, she had sobbed into Lemas' chest for half an hour before making love with him again. He was completely flummoxed.

They were back in Niemas' home, sharing Lemas' childhood bedroom, for two days before the special moot met for its first session. At Muralos' request, Lemas was present. Adara spent the first part of the day curled up in a ball in Lemas' bed, alternately sleeping and crying.

She emerged in the late afternoon, feeling half-starved and a little more sane, and sought comfort from Niemas. "I'm not really Lemas' consort," she confessed tearfully. "We've been lovers, and I was his first. But I told him from the beginning I would not stay with him, would not bear his children."

He squeezed her hands, his beautiful face full of sympathy. "And now?" he asked softly.

"Prizal… I don't know, there's something wrong with my mind," Adara admitted. "If Lemas asked me to stay with him, to bear his children and raise them, I would do it in a heartbeat. I truly love him, I think I've loved him from the first moment I saw him. But this is something else. I wear an ancient magical artifact, a necklace that is supposed to shield me from all magic. But the magic of Prizal doesn't act on me, it has acted on Lemas. And somehow, his magically-enhanced charisma gets right through my defenses. I feel I am no more immune to Lemas' charm than anyone, as if my brain had been turned off. I can't stand it much longer."

Niemas nodded soberly. He had always seemed a lightweight, an airy soul who floated along on a cloud of aesthetic joy. Undoubtedly it was Diurla's astonishing beauty that had captured his interest. But Adara saw now that he had a mind, and a sharp one. "The power of Prizal is of immense value to the merudur people," he said. "I'm sorry that it has spoiled what you and Lemas had together. But you knew that it could not last, did you not?"

Tears streaking her cheeks, Adara nodded slightly and Niemas took her into his arms and embraced her gently. There was nothing sexual in it. "Things are coming to an end," he murmured softly. "Soon, this will all be over."

It was over sooner than she expected. That night, Lemas returned to report that the special moot had voted to select a new king. The possibility existed that King Tersin would be reinstated for a further hundred-year term, but that was only a technicality. Tomorrow, nominations would be placed. He had already addressed the moot, and reactions to everything he'd had to say had been positive. Of course.

The following day, Adara and Malika walked together along the shore while Lemas returned to the moot. The semigryph's carefree attitude toward life helped her to rise above her misery, the constant battle between her heart and her mind that was tearing her apart. They were out all day, walking for miles (technically, Malika mostly flew but returned frequently to her companion), and came back to Niemas' home near suppertime to learn that Lemas had been nominated by more than one clan. That this should have happened to a barely-adult merudur youth with a tainted heritage was beyond any precedent, and Adara's sense of impending doom deepened.

That night, after making love, Adara once again pressed herself into Lemas' side. "I love you, Lemas," she said. Something she had said to Ferdyn, once.

"I love you too, Adara," he replied, drawing her into his strong arms for a deep hug. She felt as if she were drowning.

"The sword's gift," she choked out, trying to make him understand, "it's destroying my mind. I can't be your consort, can't grow old and die to leave our children without a mother – or give you children who will die in only a few decades. But I can't resist you. The Darkshield can't protect me from my love for you. Help me, Lemas!"

He squeezed her tightly again, and kissed her forehead. "Don't worry, Adara," he promised softly, "everything will be all right." His power to override her good sense kicked in again, and she melted into his arms with tears in her eyes. Not since the night the Swinzen had come to kick in the door of her childhood home had she felt so utterly helpless.

The following day was to be the first day of the voting, on a field of more than a dozen nominees out of the two hundred seventeen merudur clans. Some of the more remote clans, long since reconciled to having no political power in Elyrion, had not even bothered to send their chieftains to the moot.

Adara dragged herself out of bed after Lemas had saddled up and left for Prizlion. He could have been quartered at the Clan House, but would not consider her suggestion that he stay there until the moot was over. He wanted to be by her side, holding her in his arms. And when he was, she was unable to do anything but love him hopelessly. The more distance there was between them, though, the more like herself she began to feel.

Diurla had absented herself, gone to stay for a few days with friends in the capital. Adara suspected she was trying to avoid her stepson. If she'd resented Lemas even as a boy for being the get of her consort and the human woman he'd foolishly loved, how it must rankle her now to be near him and feel the pull of that magically-endowed charisma. Adara *loved* him, had loved him since before the sword had taken over his life, and *she* could scarcely stand it.

Niemas was sympathetic and kind, but he had no answers for her. How could he censure his son, when he himself had fallen into the same trap of love? Adara skipped breakfast and shared lunch with her host, then went out walking on the beach. Should she just run away? No, she could not. Just the thought of leaving Lemas filled her almost with panic.

Breathing the brisk salt air and watching Malika's antics as she dived for fish or tried to catch sea birds shook Adara out of her funk, and a smile touched her lips for the first time in days. Then suddenly she heard a voice calling "Adara! Adara!" She looked to her right and saw Lemas, dressed in a fine-looking robe, hurrying toward her across the strand.

She rose to her feet, a look of anxiety on her features. He came up and took her hands in his, looking into her eyes. "Did you… Are you…?" Adara choked out.

"Yes, I am to be Elyrion's new king, for a term of one hundred years beginning at my coronation three days hence. I'll be moving into the palace." She threw her arms around him and buried her face in his chest, hugging him hard. "Adara, come with me," Lemas said softly. He disentangled himself from her and took her by the hand. Calling Malika with her mind, she went with him up the trail to the house, and down the hall to his bedroom.

What, he wanted to celebrate being named king by having sex? That was a little uncharacteristic. But then everything Lemas had said and done since picking up that damned sword had been uncharacteristic. She wanted him, of course, as much as he wanted her. She'd lusted after him from the moment she had laid eyes on him, those few weeks ago at Falodar's forge.

Lemas began kissing her hungrily, his hands running over her body beneath the dress she wore. She felt his stiff cock pressing out the robe, and it filled her with desire. Soon they were in a white-hot frenzy, peeling off their clothes, and without any of the usual preliminaries Adara lay down on the bed and opened her legs to him.

He thrust inside her eagerly. But whereas he had often been quick to come when they had sex for the first time after a period of abstinence – making up for it later with repeat performances – this time he held out. Using his cock, his mouth, his hands like a musical instrument, he played a symphony of pleasure on Adara's body. He seemed to be gripped by powerful emotion, more passion even than he had shown in the past, yet somehow he held on until she was utterly wrung out, limp as a rag after coming over and over again. At last, with a shudder, he gave up his seed – buried to the hilt in her spasming cunt.

He rolled over, taking his weight off of Adara, and held her tenderly as she snuggled beneath his arm. Blown away by the power of the experience, she was half-drifting in a dream. But slowly, she became aware that he was shaking. Adara turned her head to look at him, and was stunned to see that Lemas was crying. Great salty drops were running down his cheeks and onto her hair.

"Lemas, what's the matter love?" she asked, confused. She reached up and stroked his cheek, brushing away the tears. He struggled to sit up, wiping his eyes with his hands, and sucked in a breath. When he looked at her again the tears were gone, large luminous eyes glistening. "Wisdom," he said sadly. "It's wisdom."

Adara stared at him uncomprehendingly, and Lemas rolled out of the bed and began getting back into his underclothes and the fine robe she assumed was connected with his status as king-elect. "You need to get dressed, gather the animals, and go," he told her coolly. "Back to Carlienne, maybe back to Willoughby. The further from me and Elyrion, the better."

Now tears were starting from Adara's eyes. He did not mean to try to keep her here, to ruin both their lives with a love affair that could only end in tragedy! She was saved! And it hurt so much, she wanted to curl up into a ball and sob her heart out.

Still naked, she leaped out of the bed and flew into Lemas' arms. "Oh thank you, thank you Lemas! I love you so much!" He grimaced, not quite a wry grin. It's not every day a man can get that kind of reaction by demanding that his lover leave him.

"And I love you, Adara – truly, as I said. That's why I have to let you go. That, and the wisdom thing. It's like Prizal doesn't want to let me make another mistake in my life." Adara was putting on her underclothes, and looking around for some trousers and a shirt suitable for traveling. She'd have a few miles to ride after opening a portal to Carlienne. And she hoped that would be far enough, for now. She still had things to do in the capital.

Excitement warred with desolation as she prepared to leave. She would escape, she would get over her heartache as she had done twice before, and she would move on. Everything truly *would* be all right. The thought that she would never be able to see Lemas again, that there could never have that friends-with-benefits thing with the elven king, almost made her burst into tears again.

Soon Adara had her belongings packed, and was ready to go to the stable and prepare the animals for traveling. "You'll have your pick of merudur women for your consort, you know," she told the soon-to-be King of Elyrion as he helped her saddle the animals and load the packs onto Debardo. He smiled sadly at her.

"Right, everybody in the whole country will like me," he said resignedly. "And any woman I take for a consort will be so head-over-heels in love with me that we'll probably have more than one child. I'll be the most famous merudur monarch since Myralis."

"Don't sell yourself short," Adara said, managing a grin though her heart still ached. "I loved you before you ever picked up the sword, and there are plenty of other women who would, too. Just take your time, and choose the right one. You've got decades to find your lifelong love, and meanwhile I'll be a dusty crone. It'll give me comfort in my old age to know you're ruling here, still as beautiful as the day we met."

At that she couldn't stand it any longer, and fell into his arms to sob against his chest. She had known from the first that their love had no future, so why in all the hells did she feel so devastated? She needed to leave, and soon. "Let me say goodbye to Niemas before I go," Adara said after she'd gotten ahold of herself again.

They returned to the house and found Lemas' father at work on a nearly-completed painting. It showed Lemas and Adara standing before a backdrop of what looked like clouds over the ocean. They were both dressed in questing garb, the hilt of Prizal visible above Lemas' left shoulder while the hilt of Sierlas rose above Adara's. They stood shoulder to shoulder like staunch companions, an expression of calm determination on their faces.

"Do you like it?" he asked, turning as they came into the room. He showed no surprise to see Adara dressed for traveling. "I call it The Sword Returned. I thought maybe his majesty here could hang it in the Great Hall at the palace, as a reminder of the valiant companion who helped restore the greatest treasure of the merudur to its rightful place."

The subjects of the painting gulped and ducked their heads. Niemas clearly had a photographic memory to go with his painting skills, as he had captured them perfectly though they had not sat for it. He had seen them thus garbed only briefly, when they had returned from their expedition with the sword.

"It's amazing, Niemas," Adara said. "I'm going back to Carlienne now, but I am so very glad to have met you. And thank you for all your kindness." The painter, who had set down his palette and brush as soon as they came in, drew her to him for a gentle hug. Then he kissed her on the forehead. "Do you have room in your baggage for one more item?" he asked.

Adara nodded, and Niemas produced a small, framed painting no more than twelve by sixteen inches in size. It was a view of the villa as seen from the stables, the gardens in brilliant bloom and golden sunlight streaming from a blue sky. "You never got a chance to see the house at its best," he said. "Please keep this to remember us by."

Tears in her eyes again, Adara accepted the lovely gift and squeezed Niemas' hand. Dresan was visiting at a friend's house elsewhere along the shore, and she would not get a chance to say goodbye to him. "Tell Dresan I'm sorry I missed him," she said to Lemas as they gathered the horses and mule. Called from her slumber on a pile of hay in the stables, Malika was sitting up on Debardo's packs and looking interested.

"Please go see my grandfather and explain to him what's happened," Lemas requested. "I don't think I'm going to get the chance to complete my apprenticeship, but I know he'll be thrilled to hear that we got the sword. And it'll be a week or more at least before word of what's happening in Prizlion can reach Carlienne."

"I'll do it," Adara promised. She wrapped her arms around him and pressed herself tight against his body, feeling his cock respond beneath the robe. Ah, Lemas, you lusty boy, she thought sadly. She doubted he would be remaining celibate long, no matter his concerns about finding a merudur consort whose love for him ran deeper than what Prizal could bring him.

She opened a small portal to the countryside north and east of Carlienne and peered through it, wanting to make sure she would not be seen appearing out of thin air. Good, no one in sight. Fatiha Baba enlarged it to an opening big enough to pass Adara, both horses, the mule, and the semigryph. Then with one last kiss, she stepped through it and out of Lemas' life forever.

# Chapter 26

The moment she'd put two hundred miles' distance between herself and Lemas Adara immediately felt better. She was still filled with sadness at parting with him, and at the way their recovery of the Sword of Myralis had led to his young life being co-opted for the greater good of the merudur nation. But her love for the young elf was no longer an obsession. She had gotten out of the range of his charisma, it would seem.

After depositing Sadiq and Debardo at the King's Arms, Adara had ridden Zarhya down to the waterfront to speak with Falodar. "Adara," he said heartily. His centuries living among humankind in the capital of Tanar had eroded a lot of his natural merudur reserve. "My grandson's not with you?" he asked.

By the time Adara had finished relating her tale Falodar's forge was growing cool and the old elf's mouth was hanging open in surprise. "Lemas, king of Elyrion," he murmured. "And a pureblood elf, at that..."

"I know he'd love to see you and show you the sword, Falodar," she told him. "If you can get away from your forge for a while."

Adara considered for a few moments, then decided to throw discretion to the winds. "If you'd like," she said hesitantly, "I could open a little portal for you – perhaps in your quarters upstairs – that would let you step through to the house where Niemas resides. You could visit your son and your other grandson whenever you like, and the royal palace would only be a five-mile ride away..."

Falodar's eyes grew wide. "You are a sorceress?" he asked.

"Not exactly," Adara replied wryly. "But I have certain abilities, and that is one of them."

"I have not seen that house in centuries," the elven smith admitted. "I never lived there – it was built by my own great-grandfather, and he chose to pass it to Niemas when he died. It is an ideal location for a painter, I think." Adara could tell from the look in his eyes that he loved his artistic, romantically-inclined son deeply.

When Adara mounted Zarhya again and turned her head up the hill once more there was a small portal, no bigger than a typical merudur doorway, that opened at this end inside a closet in Falodar's living quarters and led to the tack room inside the stables at Niemas' villa. She smiled to herself with satisfaction. She herself had better stay way clear of King Lemas, but there was no reason he could not be surrounded by people who loved him.

Tying Zarhya to a hitching post, Adara rang the bell at Ferdyn's townhouse and was surprised to find it opened by the man himself – looking totally gorgeous in a pair of tight linen trousers and a flowing silk shirt. Now that he was spending all his time within easy reach of razors and mirrors, he'd taken to going clean-shaven most of the time – showing off his strong jaw to good advantage.

His eyes lit at the sight of her, and Adara made an effort to paste a smile on her face. She was immensely glad to see him, but part of that gladness was the realization that she was now in the presence of a friend – someone she could talk to about what was bothering her.

"How is it you're answering the door yourself?" Adara asked archly, trying to make light of the situation as emotions swirled within her.

"It's the servants' day off," he replied with a grin. "I'm all on my lonesome. Won't you please come in?"

She had not seen him in weeks, and time before last she had fucked him on a couch in the upstairs sitting room while thinking about Lemas. Color rose in her cheeks at the thought. Adara was a bit surprised that he was alone, really. Considering he had a libido nearly as strong as Stellan's or Lemas', and that attractive young women must surely be lined up hoping for him to bestow his favors, she'd have expected to find one or two of them draped around his ankles at all times. But several times during her stay in Carlienne a few weeks ago she had chanced by, and not once had another woman been there.

Their loss was her gain, she thought, though what she really needed right now was a shoulder to cry on. It had only been a few hours since her last passionate liaison with Lemas. Just thinking about it, and the fact that the word "last" in this context meant final, ultimate, never again, was enough to bring tears to her eyes.

Ferdyn ushered her into the downstairs parlor, and bade her sit. "I was just getting ready to start on supper," he said. "Will you join me?"

"I'd love to," she replied. She'd had nothing to eat since lunch in Elyrion, and her stomach was starting to complain.

"Come on in the kitchen," he suggested. "You can help me."

Ferdyn was a competent-enough camp cook, one of his many skills that had impressed Adara when they'd first met. The thought of some of his *other* skills that had impressed her brought another blush to her cheeks. But Adara guessed that when it came to the kind of cooking you could do in a fully-equipped kitchen in a fancy townhouse in the kingdom's capital, he might be less adept.

Adara felt some of her hovering sadness lift as she looked around the kitchen. She had not cooked any meals in this room during the two months when she and Ferdyn had lived here together. They'd been out at fancy restaurants or at lavish parties in other people's homes half the time, and the staff of servants included an excellent cook. But she did know where things were kept.

I really do enjoy cooking, she realized, as she dug into the pantry and the cold chest to see what was there. Ferdyn had found a package of crisp crackers, a wheel of soft cheese, and a bottle of red wine. He brought her a little snack as she began assembling the ingredients for an intimate supper.

Once the edge had been taken off her growing hunger, Adara focused her attention on the meal. "These lamb cutlets ought to be eaten," she said. "We can season them with some rosemary and garlic, and grill them. Maybe some roasted potatoes and steamed spinach alongside?" The cooking Nanny Selden had taught her had never been fancy, and she'd grown up with a preference for meals made with simple, fresh ingredients.

Ferdyn's eyes lit, and he kissed Adara lightly on the mouth. "You have obviously arrived on my doorstep by divine providence, here to save me from enduring my own cooking!" he exclaimed. She grinned at him. His ebullient charm was such utter bullshit, but she couldn't help loving him for it.

The meal, which was really quite delicious, had been washed down with a couple of bottles of red wine. Adara had spent most of her time telling Ferdyn about the quest for the sword – all of which had occurred since she had last seen him. Toward the end of the recitation, well-lubricated, she had at last broken down and cried.

In the morning Adara rolled over and opened her eyes. The sun must be up, for warm light was streaming in through the curtains. Ferdyn lay beside her, apparently unclothed, and she had a bit of a headache. What had happened last night?

She laid a hand on his smooth, naked shoulder, and he stirred. Warm brown eyes popped open and looked at her with a startling amount of affection. "Good morning," Ferdyn said softly. Adara blinked at him, realizing that she was wearing her underclothes.

"I… good morning," she replied. "I don't entirely remember…" He grinned at her, then leaned in and kissed her on the forehead. Why did men keep doing that to her, anyhow? Ferdyn leaned forward more and took her in his arms, a tender gesture. She realized he was wearing underdrawers, though there was a stiffness within them.

"You sort of passed out there after dinner," he told her. "I tucked you into bed, and then later I came to join you." He kissed her on the forehead again. "I'm… sorry about how painful it was for you to part with your elven lover," he said. There was almost no detectible irony. She'd parted from *him* readily enough…

"Ferdyn, I'm sorry to have burdened you," Adara said softly. "It wasn't just love, there was some kind of magic that was able to slip right past the Darkshield. I thought I was losing my mind." He gave her a little squeeze.

"So you said," he replied softly. "It's all right, 'Dara. You're free from Prizal's influence now, and you're among friends."

Adara was surprised to find that, this morning, she was able to look back on the whole experience as if from a remove – without any stabbing emotional pain. "Thank you Ferdyn," she said sincerely. "You're a true friend." She kissed him on the cheek.

"With benefits?" he replied, desire glowing in those friendly brown eyes. She pressed her lips against his, and slipped her tongue into his mouth.

The End
(For now)